Out of Time

Albert Samson, once described as the private eye combining 'the best moral qualities of the Continental Op and Lew Archer', feels life is looking good when he acquires two clients in an afternoon.

The first, an eccentric old man living in an expensive apartment and obsessed with his home computer, asks him to investigate a young man suspected of running with a wild crowd.

The second is a wealthy banker, Douglas A. Belter, whose wife has discovered that her birth certificate is a fake. For forty-eight years she'd believed herself to be the daughter of Ella and the late Earl Wilmott Murchison. Now she wonders if she has any identity at all.

The latter case intrigues Samson and his investigation leads him, via dusty archives, a sentimental night club, the police and the press, to the 1930s and '40s and to an old murder. It also leads him to suspect a recent 'natural death' is in fact a cold-blooded killing.

Michael Lewin's immaculate writing, his skill in creating character and his gift for slowly but relentlessly building tension has made *Out of Time* his strongest and most memorable novel.

MICHAEL Z. LEWIN

OUT OF TIME

An Albert Samson Mystery

NO EXIT PRESS

1989

No Exit Press
18 Coleswood Road
Harpenden, Herts AL5 1EQ

Copyright © 1984 Michael Lewin

First published in U.K. 1984 by Macmillan

British Library Cataloguing in Publication Data

Lewin, Michael Z.
  Out of time – (No Exit Press Contemporary Crime)
  I. Title
813'.54[F]

ISBN 0 948353 44 9

9 8 7 6 5 4 3 2 1

Printed by William Collins, Glasgow

To Lois Wallace,
and H. Yaffey – my best British reader

ONE

The girl sat in my outer office cum waiting room. She was fidgeting with a hanky. She ran it through the fingers of one hand, then the other.

I opened my inner office door and took one step forward. She stood up.

I said, in an earnest, utterly trustworthy way, 'My name is Albert Samson. I'm a private detective. Can I help you?'

She looked at me, but only for a moment. Her gaze dropped to my shoelaces. Despite the diffidence she was brassily beautiful. Falteringly she said, 'Oh, I hope so, I hope so!' A glance up. She fluttered her eyelids. 'But it is a personal problem. And it's so hard to know where to start.'

I stepped aside and gestured to my office. 'Why don't you come in, sit down, and start at the beginning.'

She lifted her baby blue eyes to mine and said, 'Oh thank you!' She dabbed at the eyes with the hanky. She walked into the office. I followed her and closed the door behind us.

After a long moment she opened it again.

She stood framed in the doorway, facing the camera.

She said, 'And that is how most of us picture the start of a new case for a private eye. The agitated girl, the shabby office that doubles as a home, the lone detective with his bottle of Scotch. Well, Albert Samson *is* a private detective and he does work alone, but I can tell you he hasn't offered me so much as a whiff of whiskey and he says that he's hardly ever had an agitated girl for a client. This is Tanya Wilkerson for WTRH-TV News and I'm Out and About. Most private detectives work for large agencies these days, but we've found one of the last of his breed, alive and well in our own Indianapolis. Does Albert Samson tread a noble lonely path through the maelstrom of human wickedness or is life for the modern-day dick not so glamorous as it used to be? Spend a few minutes with me in his inner sanctum and we'll find out.'

I watched the programme noble and alone. Well, not programme exactly. Two hundred and seventy-two second feature on the Monday evening WTRH news.

It hardly seemed to last a minute. The interview flew by, like my life passing before my eyes.

I needn't have been alone. I could have watched with my woman friend and her daughter. But if I was to be thrust suddenly into the forefront of local private detection, with the phone ringing so much its perch would get wobbly, I owed it to the customers to answer the calls myself.

The strategy proved to be a little optimistic. I hadn't expected sudden fame from my television spot, but . . . something.

At about nine-thirty I gave up on my silent telephone and went out to do some shopping. I spent twenty-five minutes in the supermarket and nobody looked at me twice, except when I was at the checkout. Circumstances require me to be a rather careful shopper and when I was going through my pockets to make the 20 cents on my $7.20 ticket, the bagger looked at me a second time. But I don't think it was because I'd been on TV.

When I got home I wrote Tanya a note saying how well she'd done her Out and About on me. They love flattery, show people. And who knew? Some follow-up on my more unusual cases? You have to keep irons in the fire for the future these days to keep from being overwhelmed by the cold steel of the present.

Tanya had seemed interested enough while she was with me.

How did you get into it? By a happy chain of accidents. (While eliminating all the good occupations.)

Is it interesting work? A lot more often than you might think. (Once a year.)

Do you get a lot of satisfaction out of it? It's very fulfilling to give a client a full report on what he or she wants to know. (And to get a cheque, and have a square meal.)

Do you carry a gun? No, I don't even own one. (Which hasn't kept me from being shot at a few times.)

Can you really make a living at it these days? I've been at it for years and I'm still here. (Ignoring the detail that I pay no rent because I have a deal with my landlord to double as a watchman for his premises and a large quantity of plate glass he stores out back.)

Do you meet a lot of sexy women? I'm not one to kiss and tell. (Or even to kiss, if it comes to that.)

If any of our viewers have problems they think you could help with, do you have time at the moment to take on any extra work? I always have time to talk to people and advise them whether their problem is the kind I think I can be of help with or not. (Thank you, blessed Tanya, for asking like I asked you to.)

I don't know whether anybody watches WTRH. But they won't hold Tanya Wilkerson long. She's too good. She spent fifteen minutes just rehearsing her fidgeting.

The next morning I got three calls as a result of my commercial.

They restored my faith in the American way of life.

The first was from a man who identified himself as Douglas A. Belter. He said he would like to consult me

9

about a personal matter.

I said I would be happy to meet him.

What had been a conversation conducted in measured and businesslike tones then became hesitant. He said, 'I . . . . Because of the nature of the situation would it . . . ? Might I see you out of office hours?'

I offered six p.m. He agreed immediately.

As I entered the appointment in my notebook, I felt I knew the name in a vague sort of way. But it stayed vague.

The second call came an hour later while I was getting my dirty clothes together. A male voice asked, 'Mr Samson?'

'Speaking.'

'Saw you on the box last night.'

'Oh?'

'Turned my stomach. All that soft soap about taking an interest in clients as people. Steering them to somebody else if their problem is something you can't handle. You defectives are all the same. What a load of ball bearings.'

'It's nice weather for December,' I said. 'Why don't you take a hike?'

I hung up.

Tanya warned me I might get nuisance calls.

I sat a minute thinking about my laundry. Trying to remember whether this was the month to sort it into whites and colours or the month for synthetics and naturals. With the holidays coming there would be social commitments. The decision could be important.

The phone rang again.

When I answered it a man said, 'Mr Samson, I saw you on television last night.'

'I'd love to chat,' I said, 'but I'm up to my neck in filthy business here. If you have anything serious to say, then get on with it. Otherwise buzz off.'

There was a long pause.

He said, 'If you introduce yourself to all prospective clients this way, I'm surprised you make any kind of living at all.' About this time I realised I was talking to a new caller.

I began to waffle about crank calls.

Coldly he said, 'I have a job which I would like to talk to you about. My name is Normal Bates. I live in Tarkington Tower. Do you know it?'

'Yes,' I said.

'1203. At three.'

Despite myself as I put the receiver down I felt cheerful, thinking that my personal economic recession might be about to break. Maybe I would lead the country back to prosperity.

I put the answering machine on and went out to the launderette. Mid-cycle I did the dutiful thing and called my mother, who runs a diner on the near-Southside. She said that she hadn't seen me on the television herself, but a friend had and I had seemed 'sweet'.

Even that didn't get me down.

TWO

Tarkington Tower is on the near-Northside, an early effort at the kind of gentrification of a downtown area which has been pursued with intensity more recently by local politicians and businessmen.

We're awash with new buildings and projects in Indianapolis just now, attempts to divert some of the mainstream of national events, attention and prestige from other centres. A lot of rich and powerful people are deeply involved. I think it is a good thing: it gives them something to do and keeps them off the streets. There's nothing more dangerous than rich and powerful people with time on their hands.

I arrived at Tarkington Tower at two fifty-five. It is twelve stories high and the elevator worked. My rates and hopes rose with each passing floor.

I rang the bell of 1203. Within a few seconds it opened wide to reveal an old man with bright eyes and a horseshoe of white hair making a ringer on his pate. He wore plaid braces which blazed on the background of a plain white shirt. The braces supported trousers which didn't know whether to cover or reveal the extent of a substantial pot belly. Compromise ruled and they came up half way.

'The famous Mr Samson,' he said.

'And you are Mr Bates.'

'Come in. Sit down.'

12

He led me slowly but very surely down a short hall. We arrived in a sitting room, large but sparsely furnished. He settled into the one upholstered chair. It was squarely before a window that filled the entire outside wall of the room. Unexpectedly, he rotated on a masked swivel to look at the view.

There was no obvious place for me to sit, so I moved the only other chair in the room from its location in front of a home computer at a side wall. The computer was on. The screen read, 'Talk to me, baby.'

I put the chair so it faced Bates and I sat down.

The other furnishings in the room were a four-tier bookshelf on the wall opposite the computer and a floor-to-ceiling rubber plant near the entrance to a kitchenette.

Bates said nothing, so I too turned to the window. It overlooked central Indianapolis to the south and there couldn't have been more than a dozen places in town with comparable vistas. Exciting even on a grey day.

'My city,' Bates said. 'My city.'

Then he turned to face me. 'So you're a private eye.' His eyes, seen again, appeared almost to glow.

'I am indeed,' I said.

'Are you good?'

'I do what I can.'

'There is a man I would like you to investigate for me. Can you do that?'

'It depends what kind of investigation you want. I can't follow him for twenty-four hours a day myself, for instance. Though I can have it done.'

'There may be some surveillance involved, but that's not the essential part. Go over to the computer, will you?'

I went to the computing rig.

'Type "Lance Whisstock".'

I typed Lance Whisstock.

'Now hit the "enter" key.'

13

I hit enter.

The screen came to life, displaying a collection of facts headed, 'Lance Whisstock'. They were things like age, height and weight; where and when he had been to college; that he was divorced; and that he was such a good baseball player that he had been drafted as a pitcher by the Padres when he was in high school.

Bates said, 'Now hit the "F-1" key, type "Print" and enter it.'

The machine accepted my instructions and clattered into life. It printed me a paper copy of what had just been displayed on the screen. I tore it off and came back to my chair.

'Love these newfangled things,' Bates said with a smile. 'I've been thinking about having an ear pierced, but can't make up my mind which one.'

'I think you're joshing me, Mr Bates.'

'Maybe a little.'

I looked at him and asked, 'So, what is the story?'

'The boy is the grandson of a friend of mine, and he seems to have gone off the rails. Hanging out with a lot of low-lifes. My friend is worried and I said I would try to find out what was up with the kid. That's about it.'

'I see,' I said.

'I've got a photograph of the boy,' Bates said, and from a shirt pocket he took a snapshot and handed it to me. 'Got a longer beard and longer hair now, but you ought to recognise him from that.'

The picture was of a dark burly man who looked older than the twenty-six I knew him to be from the data sheet.

'You must be a pretty good friend of the grandfather to go to all this trouble,' I said.

'I try to be a good friend,' Bates said forcefully. 'Choose 'em carefully, and stick by 'em. That's the rule I've gone by and it's never let me down yet. You know how old I am, Mr

Samson?'

'I wouldn't want to guess,' I said.

'I'll be seventy-six years old next March.'

He didn't look it. 'You certainly don't look it,' I said.

'And if I had one bit of advice to give to a young man it would be to stick by his friends.'

I nodded.

'But maybe you'll be happier to take this than advice.' He took a folded cheque from his pocket. 'A little retainer.'

I tried to exercise self-control as I accepted it. It's not polite to grab.

'His grandfather says that Lance has been spending time in the bars along Illinois, south of Fall Creek. They had a talk in The Fandango a couple of weeks ago. You might well pick him up around there.'

'Not the most salubrious part of town,' I said.

'No,' Bates said.

'You don't have things like a home address?'

'Nor a place of work.'

'I could go a long time without finding him.'

'I understand that. And I understand that you may well have other commitments.'

I shrugged agreement. One can hope.

'I would like you to report to me frequently, however, even if you are not getting anywhere. My friend is anxious. If I can tell him I've talked to you each day, he'll feel better.'

'All right, Mr Bates. But are you aware how private detectives operate? I do have a few friends of my own, but no special connections that will provide all the information you might want by noon tomorrow. You might do better, or faster, by hiring one of the big agencies.'

'Thank you for the suggestion,' he said. 'But you'll do.'

I headed towards home from Tarkington Tower, but by

way of Illinois Street. There is a mile or so where the bars are numerous and the reputation is bad. Not the only place in town where the rougher gays get together or where you can buy chemical highs without American Express, but it's not the kind of area you'd like your grandchild to spend its time. Not the same grandchild you dandled on your knee and dressed up as Santa Claus for.

The only stop I made on the way back to the office was to deposit the cheque.

When I got in I found a message on the answering machine. When I played it back, the message was a request that I call a Mr Lyon at 547 3577. The caller spelled the name.

I hummed as I hung my coat up and mused about getting myself a new one for Christmas. Depositing cheques, even small ones, has that kind of effect on me. I dialled the number and then listened to myself ask for Mr Lyon while I was absorbing that the answering voice had said, 'Indianapolis Zoo.'

A little joke.

Thank you someone.

I felt suddenly tired.

THREE

Douglas A. Belter was on time to the second by his Swiss pocket chronometer. He arrived in the only bespoke-tailored three-piece suit that had ever walked into premises of mine. The suit was a fine grey number which toned in with his carefully coiffed fine grey hair. He had grey eyes and a grey face. The only break in the cloudy exterior was the gold chain which led to the watch in his waistcoat pocket.

I knew he was on time because he was holding the timepiece in his left hand as he came through the door and he said, 'On time. I was afraid I was going to be late.'

I was sitting in the outer office. 'Busy day?' I asked conversationally.

'They all are,' he said without trace of even a social smile. 'Douglas A. Belter.' He advanced on me with his right hand extended.

What could I do?

'Albert Samson.' I rose and shook the hand.

And I placed the name. There were Belters in Indianapolis who were bankers and who appeared on social pages. Sometimes, when I am not rushed off my feet with work, I read the paper thoroughly.

'Are you one of the banking Belters?' I asked.

'I am,' he said. 'But this is a personal matter. Where do we talk?'

I led him to the inner office, as advertised on television. I felt like a beer, but couldn't go to the ice box without offering him one. And he just didn't strike me as beer.

He looked to be in his late forties. Although I had sailed through a few of my fifth decade birthdays without threatening a soul, they are said to be a man's dangerous years. I wondered if he had been dating a teenager and was now being blackmailed by the girl's greedy granny.

My mind sometimes goes on idle flights after six.

Belter settled himself in my client's chair and then took a deep breath. 'I need,' he said, 'to be certain of the confidentiality of what I say to you.'

'I can cross my heart,' I said, 'but you'll only get full confidentiality if I am employed by a lawyer on your behalf.'

'I don't want other people brought into this,' Belter said firmly. 'Which is one of the reasons I have come to someone who works on his own.'

'And out of business hours, so it's not in your secretary's diary.'

'Correct,' he said, and raised an eyebrow.

I shrugged. 'A P.I. stands to lose his licence if he tells anyone besides his client what he's learned on a case. Except reporting criminality to the police. I've held my licence a lot of years.'

'But will you be discreet?' he said quickly, though I thought I'd already promised as much.

I get tense when a man in a three-piece suit begins to fuss. 'You wouldn't like a beer, would you?'

He blinked. 'A beer would be very welcome,' he said.

Because he hadn't loosened his tie, I poured it into glasses.

'Thank you,' he said as I gave him his.

We both sat and we both drank.

'What's the problem?' I asked.

18

He looked at his glass. He said, 'My wife and I will have been married for twenty-five years in June. The plan was, is, to take a special anniversary trip and spend eight weeks in Europe. Over the years we've been to most parts of this country, the places that are interesting for vacationers. Followed the "see America first" maxim. But the idea this time was to do something special. Go to Cab's graduation – that is our younger son, who finishes at Yale this year. Then, straight on, to Europe. Our first time, ever, abroad.'

'Sounds very nice,' I said, thinking of my own daughter finishing college in Austria.

'We went to get our passports yesterday,' Belter said.

I waited.

'And they wouldn't issue one to my wife.'

'Why not?'

'The official said that her birth certificate was not valid.'

My face showed my surprise.

'There was some irregularity about the impress.'

I frowned. 'They said it was a forgery?'

'They didn't use that word. But that's what they meant. The man we saw was really quite nice about it. He said almost anyone else would have passed it, but he makes a collection of such things. He even showed us a sample of pre-war impresses. Ours was clearly different.'

'What's the history of the certificate?' I asked.

'My wife's mother gave it to her when we got our marriage licence. It's been sitting in my personal documents file ever since.'

'Was the certificate the original or a copy?'

'The original as far as we knew.'

'And it was a surprise to your wife?'

'A complete shock and puzzle,' Belter said with sympathy. 'She nearly broke down when the official told us. I've tried to reassure her that it is bound to have been a clerical mistake, but she's been in something of a daze since

19

she left the passport office. I would have stayed home from work today, except we have a housekeeper who has been with us for years and is, as they say, one of the family.'

'And you've been tracking down the clerical mistake,' I said.

'Yes. I went back to the original records.'

'And?'

'Marion County Birth Certificates Office on Ohio Street has no record of my wife being born.'

'She was born in Marion County?'

'Supposedly.'

'When did you go?'

'Yesterday. After the Passport Office.'

'Both of you?'

'No. I sent Paula home. She is rather volatile at the best of times. Something of an artistic temperament.'

'Did you tell her about your visit to the Birth Certificates Office?'

'I told her what I knew at the time, last night. That they were making a thorough check, but certainly didn't have her listed with the details on the certificate we have.'

'What did she say?'

'She didn't know what to say. Except that she wants it unravelled.'

'Does she know you've come to me?'

'We talked last night in the kitchen while Tamae was making dinner.'

'Tamae is your housekeeper?'

'Housekeeper plus. Yes. She has a little television in there and it was on. We saw you on the news. Paula said we better hire you to find out whether she had ever been born or whether she was just a figment of my imagination. So I said I would. I don't know whether she took me seriously.'

'Did *you* take you seriously?'

'Yes,' he said gravely. 'The Birth Certificate people say

20

that no one was born with Paula's name or to Paula's mother any time within three years either side of the date we have.'

Belter and I shared a quiet moment, each finishing his drink.

I explained what it would cost to have me go into things and he just nodded. Not exactly the stiff negotiation that has been my experience of bankers.

'You got the certificate from your wife's mother?'

'That's right.'

'Is she still alive?'

'Oh yes.'

I hadn't expected that answer.

'Why don't you just go ask her?' I held my hands up. 'Don't tell me. You did.'

'Yes. This afternoon.'

I waited for a moment. 'Mr Belter, come on. Is this going to be the shortest period of employment on record or not? What did she say?'

'My mother-in-law is eighty-seven and has been in a twenty-four-hours-a-day nursing establishment for six years. She has times when she is completely lucid. In fact, she is quite remarkable for her age. But at other times she is not aware of what is going on around her. For instance, she has a recurrent delusion that people are trying to poison her and when it has a grip, visiting can be quite an ordeal. That's the way she was today. I didn't get any useful information at all.'

I thought for a moment.

'How long do the delusionary episodes generally last?'

'It's hit and miss. I don't want to wait around, doing nothing. She might not be willing to help even if lucid. Given,' he said slowly, 'that she is inescapably involved in whatever deception has been perpetrated.'

'You don't think it possible that there is some innocent

21

explanation?'

'With a faked birth certificate?' The grey eyes flashed steely. 'We only avoided being faced with charges of trying to obtain a passport with false documents because Paula was so patently shocked.'

I said, 'Wherever your wife was born, there is very probably a record of it. Either she was born outside Marion County or she was born in Marion County but under a different name. In either case, it looks like the thing for me to do is to try to work back through your wife's family history to try to reconstruct what the circumstances of the birth were. Is your wife's father alive?'

'No. He died in the war,' Belter said. 'The putative father.'

'Will your wife help establish dates and places?'

'Yes,' he said without uncertainty.

'All right. Would you ask her to assemble a chronology, as best she can, of where her parents lived, what kind of work they did? Anything that might have left records. And of course I'll need their name.'

'Murchison,' he said.

I turned my notebook to a fresh page. 'Give me what you know now, off the top. To get me started.'

Before he left, Belter also gave me a retainer.

I could hardly contain myself as he went out the door. They do late banking at the establishment where I conduct my financial transactions. Not a Belter Bank. I drove the five blocks and deposited the day's second cheque with a nonchalance intended to suggest that it was a routine chore for me. I left deeply disappointed that I hadn't been observed making the deposits by one of the branch management's upper echelon. I am known to them.

Still, at seven-fifteen bank people tend to be at home planning their vacations and talking in front of their housekeepers about whether their wives' parents are concealing genealogical secrets.

I went to a supermarket outside of which I telephoned to offer to share my boost in fortune with my lady friend, to the tune of a good steak, with a nut cutlet thrown in for her now vegetarian daughter. But she didn't hear my melody. No one answered the phone.

I bought a TV dinner and went home.

While it was cooking I went to work. I commissioned background research on Lance Whisstock and on the Murchison family.

My contact, Maude Simmons, works on the Sunday *Star* and supplements her income by searching the *Star* clipping files, in her spare moments, on behalf of folks like me. She's also got eyes and ears all around town, an audio-visual Hydra. When I have the money for her service, she does quickly a lot of things I can only do slowly.

I ate my TV dinner in the self-righteous knowledge that I actually was hard at work. It allowed me to savour every mouthful.

FOUR

In the morning I went to Biarritz House, a nursing home on Graceland Avenue, north of 38th Street. It was a large white-frame structure in comfortable grounds which looked just like a high-class nursing home should. And nothing but high class would be appropriate for a Belter Mother-In-Law.

I didn't know much about Ella R. Murchison. Most of the information Belter had given me had been about his wife, Paula, and himself.

Until the previous day, he had 'known' that his wife was the Murchisons' only child, and that they had been long-time residents of Indianapolis. He had met Paula when she was nineteen and had played in a piano recital of the students of Louis Dettlaff, then a prominent instructor of the keyboard arts. Belter's younger sister had also played. Douglas was introduced at a reception after the performance. It was in May of 1955.

They were married in June of 1957. Belter's impression was that his wife's family was hard up before the war, but better off afterwards. Certainly when he met Paula, she and her mother lived comfortably enough, in a small house on 42nd Street, just east of Central. She'd had a good piano at home, and lessons with Dettlaff didn't come cheap. Paula had attended School 60, at 46th and Central from the fifth grade, and then Shortridge High School. Belter didn't

24

remember the home address on 42nd, but would be able to recognise the house. He recalled its proximity both to a library branch and to the Uptown Cinema on College.

All he knew about the Murchisons before the war was that they had lived in a different house, and that Earl W. had held a variety of jobs before joining the Army. He had died on the way to Europe in 1942 in some sort of shipboard accident. For whatever reason, Paula had told her husband comparatively little about her early childhood.

I parked in the Biarritz drive and at about a quarter past ten I asked at the central desk for Mrs Murchison.

'My my,' said the gently southern accented nurse. 'What a lucky lady our Ella is.'

I began to preen in the face of unwonted flattery when the nurse made clear what she meant. 'That makes three visitors for her in two days. Could you go down there and ask for Mrs Howard, please, honey.'

She pointed. I went.

Mrs Howard was not gently accented. She was forward and bustly and warm and left her menu planning to take me to the room.

As we walked along the corridor, I asked easily, 'How is Mrs Murchison today?'

'Oh, fine.'

'I was talking to Doug, Mr Belter, and he said that yesterday she was off about poisoning again.'

'We're all Borgias here from time to time,' Mrs Howard said with a smile.

'It must be difficult when she's minded that way,' I said.

'We get our fill of "poison tasting",' she said. 'But generally in the end we leave the food on her table and go away. When we come back it's gone. Now, I can't testify that she eats it, but she's not exactly wasting away, our Ella.'

25

'Do all the residents eat in their rooms?'

'No, no. But she fell twice a couple of weeks ago so we're being a bit careful.'

We stopped in front of a door marked '23'. Mrs Howard knocked, paused and went in. 'Another visitor for you, Ella. A young gentleman. Are you decent?'

Mrs Howard waved me to follow her into the room and pointed to a chair near the bay window which surveyed large landscaped gardens at the back of the house.

Ella Murchison sat in another chair facing the window. She was crocheting, and glanced towards me and Mrs Howard brightly. A substantial woman, she looked fifteen years younger than her advertised age.

'This is Mr Samson,' Mrs Howard said. 'He knows your Douglas and your Paula too, I shouldn't wonder. I'll be back a little later on.'

Mrs Howard left.

Ella Murchison did not return to her work. She watched me carefully as I sat down.

'Hello,' I said cheerfully.

'I don't know you,' she said.

She was not in doubt.

'No,' I said.

'You're not that young. Are you a gentleman?'

'I try to say my please and thank yous.'

'Mrs Howard says that you know Douglas and Paula. Do you know my grandsons too?'

'I've heard a little about them. And I haven't met Paula yet.'

She picked up her crochet work and began hooking the yarn dexterously.

'It's very pretty,' I said. 'What is it going to be?'

She didn't answer at first. Then she put the work down, faced me again and said, 'What do you want, Mr Samson?'

All notions of possible indirections departed. 'Your

26

son-in-law has hired me,' I said.

'To keep me company?' she said without laughing. 'What a kind and thoughtful boy he is.'

'Not to keep you company,' I said.

She plumped up her hair with her two hands. 'If I'm going to have company, I should get myself ready.'

'He's worried about your daughter.'

'You may not think me much to look at now,' Mrs Murchison said, 'but in my day I had looks. Oh yes. Not bad in my day.'

I stopped talking.

She said, 'There's one or two old codgers in this place who don't think I'm so bad even now, you know. You look surprised.'

'No, I don't.'

'Well, be surprised as you like. It's true.' She looked at me sharply. 'You haven't brought me any chocolates, have you?'

'No,' I said.

'Fancy that. Visiting a lady without bringing her anything. Some of my old gentlemen buy me chocolates every week, out of their pocket money. But I don't touch them.' She bent forward and narrowed her eyes. 'They put things in those chocolates. They do. You can scoff. You can mock. But I'm on to their little game. So, no sooner do the boxes come in than they go out. Straight in the basket. They can't fool me that way. Not me.'

She stopped talking and picked up her crochet work again.

I sat quietly with her for a long couple of minutes.

Finally, I tried again. 'Paula is upset,' I said.

Mrs Murchison didn't take her eyes off her work. 'So, don't you try to get into my good books by bringing me candy another time. I'm too smart for that. Too smart.'

I rose and went to the door. I opened it, and then closed

27

it without going out.

Immediately the old woman lowered her hands and turned with a sigh. When she saw me still standing in the room her reaction was fierce. 'What are you trying to trick me like that for? You think it's goddamn funny to play pranks on old women? You get out of here.'

I nodded, and left.

Mrs Howard was in the foyer talking to the nurse at reception. She turned to me as I approached. 'Has she sent you to get something?'

'No,' I said. 'I'm on my way.'

'That wasn't much of a visit,' Mrs Howard said, with a practised tone of faint criticism.

'It seemed to be as much as she wanted,' I said.

The southern nurse said, 'She had two visitors yesterday, Connie.'

Mrs Howard said, 'Really?'

'Yes, honey. That Chinese housekeeper of her daughter's, and then her son-in-law. I'd think she was just about visited out.'

Mrs Howard said to me, 'I was off yesterday.'

'She got on to poisons,' I said.

Both women laughed briefly. Then Mrs Howard shrugged. 'She ate breakfast this morning without a word.'

'I didn't feel it was a delusion,' I said.

'What do you mean?' Mrs Howard asked. 'That someone *is* poisoning her?'

'I felt she turned it on, so as not to talk to me. She seemed very alert. Much younger than her years.'

Both women nodded in agreement. I asked, 'Does she get a lot of visitors?'

'Oh, the family's quite good. Daughter, grandchildren, pretty regularly,' Mrs Howard said.

'And the Chinese housekeeper,' the nurse said.

'I think she's Japanese, Barbara.'

'Oh my!' the nurse said. 'Anyway, she comes too.'

'Three or four times a month, I'd say. Oh, they're not bad. They bring her things. Books and magazines, yarn, tapes of concerts sometimes. They're musical, you know. Definitely among our good relatives.' She looked at the nurse. 'What percentile would you say?'

After a moment's thought the nurse said, 'Nothing like the Grosses or the Fallowfields, of course. But . . . top twenty?'

Mrs Howard nodded. Then to me she said, 'Maybe if you come back in a couple of days she'll be more receptive. Unless visiting again would be too inconvenient for you.'

The burden of retaining the Belter top-twenty rating was squarely on my shoulders.

I was on the road again by eleven. By pre-arrangement I was to call Maude Simmons between eleven and half past. Where better to make a telephone call than from a pay phone at the Indiana Bell office on North Meridian?

Maude sounded tired. 'I've only had time for the information off the surface. The one-cut skim. You understand that?'

'Yes.'

'O.K. Just checking.'

'A girl's got to keep things straight,' I said.

'Yeah,' she said, acknowledging unspecified stresses. 'A girl sure has.'

I've known Maude superficially for years, primarily through this sort of occasional commercial relationship. I know little about her, except that she has an unquenchable thirst for funds from which she seems to enjoy no material benefit. Some day, if I get rich, I'll ask her for background on herself. And she'll give it to me, if I pay.

'I didn't come up with anything at all on a Lance Whisstock in the newspaper files, but I haven't gone for court records on his divorce. You want those?'

'I think so.' They would, at least, give me a former address and a former wife.

'And how about high school and college transcripts?'

'Yeah, those too.'

'And you didn't give me anything about parents.'

'I don't have anything about parents.'

'You don't have a lot, do you?'

'I hope you don't intend to charge me for that newsflash,' I said.

'Now, Murchison. Speaking of whom, there's not a lot on them either. Almost nothing on the mother and father, and little enough on Paula Helen.'

'Let's hear about Paula Helen.'

'I've got some piano concerts in the mid-fifties. You want to know what she played?'

'No.'

'Then she married Douglas Alan Belter, second son of Steven G. Belter. You know who he is?'

'Yes. Banks, not piggy.'

'Six branches in town, plus a few elsewhere in the state. I can give you a lot on the father.'

'No.'

'Douglas is in the business. Married Paula Helen June the first, 1957. Tabernacle Presbyterian on East 34th. She was twenty-one. He was twenty-two. You want the guest list? The menu?'

'How about sending me a copy of the guest list?'

'O.K.'

'There must have been something about her parents in the wedding story.'

'"The bride's mother is Ella R. Murchison, widow of Earl Wilmott Murchison."'

'Very revealing,' I said.

'Must have been love,' Maude said. 'No list of any

30

domains Princess Paula brought to the kingdom.'

'Wonderful thing, love.'

'The Douglas Belters are social. Musical associations. Charitable money. There's a lot of it, but nothing looks special. I can make copies and send them too.'

'All right.'

'Children: two sons. Raymond William in '59, Charles Arthur in '61. I haven't looked for items on them.'

'That's all right.'

'It's not very exciting, Al.'

'If I want things in more detail, I'll get back to you.'

'I hear you looked lovely on TV,' she said. 'Didn't get to see you myself, but they say you came across like a fine wine.'

She waited a moment for me to rise to the bait, but I was silent.

'Full-bodied. Must have done business a power of good.'

'I had a couple of calls.' Not counting Mr Lyon.

'How did you find Tanya Wilkerson?'

'All right,' I said.

'Word is she's a real bitch when you get to know her. But destined for big things.'

'I'll try not to be hurt when I get left behind.'

'Gotta go.'

She went.

From the phone booth it was only a few steps to the Reception Desk of the Indiana Bell Administration office.

A serious young man in a dark suit sat before a glass case of speciality telephones which ranged from a push-button Micky Mouse to a model with built-in scrambler, not usually needed by politicians.

'May I help you?'

'I'd like to see the telephone books for 1934 through 1947 please,' I said.

31

As he stared at me, I thought I heard a million synapses open and close. But finally he said, 'You'll want our Archives office. Third and fourth floors.'

The Archivist was genuinely pleased to see me. 'It's all part of my job,' he said, 'to assist with public and commercial enquiries.'

'Oh, good.'

'And schools,' he said with enthusiasm. He was a small bald man with bristles coming out of all sorts of places.

He led me to shelves which bore Indianapolis telephone directories through the ages. 'We have the only complete set of these books in existence,' he said proudly. 'Some were pretty hard to locate.'

'Do many people use them?'

'I've had a few, a few,' he said. 'Will you be able to finish your work today?'

'It should only take a few minutes,' I said.

'Oh,' he said, clearly disappointed. 'Good.'

It only took a few minutes.

I'd come to the books on the off-chance that the Murchisons before the war had telephones. They did, and to simplify matters they had only one listed address, on East New York Street, for the years 1934 through 1945. In 1946 the address changed, to East 42nd Street, and for the first time the listing was under Ella R. instead of Earl W.

While I was about it I went farther back in time. 1932 was the first year for the New York Street address. There were no phone numbers for either Murchison back through 1920.

I returned to the Archivist. 'They've been a great help,' I said.

I seemed to have made his day.

Then I unmade it. 'Do you have a copy of the current directory?'

32

'The current one?'

'Like, this year's,' I said.

'What for?'

'I want to look up a number.'

'That's not what they're here for,' he said sternly.

Over-harsh, I thought. Perhaps he thought so too, because he relented and fished a directory out of the desk drawer.

I leafed through to the Whisstocks. There was only one and that one not a Lance. I copied down the address and number, thanked the Archivist fulsomely, and left.

Since I was already in town, I parked at the Market Square lot and ventured into the Indianapolis Police Department.

I made for the Detective day room on the third floor. From the reception I learned that Lieutenant Jerry Miller was, indeed, in his cubbyhole.

'Don't let him know I'm coming,' I said. 'He might leave.'

The officer shrugged. He didn't care.

When Miller saw me he didn't complain, make a face, bury his head in a desk drawer, or jump out the window.

It was a sign that things were not well with him.

He put his pen down and rose. 'It's about lunch time, Al,' he said. 'What say we go out for a bite?'

He spoke as if it were a routine activity. I hardly remembered when I last ate lunch with the man. Though we were friends in high school, we've let social contacts lapse more recently. I visit him at work. And he is generally suspicious that I want something from him. Which, generally, I do.

'Great,' I said.

We went to a deli stand in City Market, across Market Street from the cop shop. We carried sandwiches and coffee

33

and walked the sawdust-strewn aisles separating the sale of fish and meat and vegetables, leather work and used paperbacks and plastic toys.

At one point Miller's gaze lingered on some candy canes in a confectionery display. I bought a couple and he seemed joyful.

He talked non-stop.

He talked about how he'd like to run a stand in the Market, but the waiting list was too long. He talked about some vacations he'd taken visiting family in Nebraska. How he had a cousin there with a plan to exploit Nebraska's tourist potential. With an option on a lake. With zoning permission to build a road.

He talked about how much like his wife, Janie, his young daughter was already. 'It's uncanny,' he said.

It was not an observation which brought him pleasure.

I hadn't seen Janie for more than 'Hello' for years, because she doesn't like me. She remembers doggedly the days when Jerry and I chummed up at school, and joy rode a time or two. She is highly ambitious for her husband.

'It's a hell hole in there,' he said suddenly. I realised he meant at work. 'There's so much angling, dirty dealing. For promotion, for assignments, for funds, for manpower. Putting other guys down. Putting yourself and your friends up.' He shook his head. 'The biggest danger a working cop in this city runs is from a knife in the back at work.'

We stopped at a stand selling dried fruit, nuts, grains and health food.

'You ever try this stuff? he asked.

'Not in a big way.'

'Maybe I will. I need something.' He turned to me. 'What did you want, Al? Something big, I hope?'

I looked surprised. I was surprised. Our history, since we went our career ways, has been of me having to use dynamite to prise even little favours from the man. He has

34

high principles about what is right and what is wrong. Since he got the religion of being a policeman.

He saw my reaction. He smiled without happiness and lifted his shoulders. 'I need a big case,' he said simply, 'if I'm not going to get stuck forever. If I'm not going to get farmed out to make way for the college-boy hot shots, I need to deliver. Hell, I *do* deliver, but I need a big case for decoration. You've done that for me a time or two over the years.'

He turned to walking the aisles again. Then he slapped me on the back. 'Doesn't have to be a mass murderer,' he said jovially. 'Baby-snatching, gang incest, or even a white-slavery ring will do. Hey, that'd give some nice visuals for the papers and TV. Stand me up with the white slave I've rescued.'

Miller is black.

'You might take your life savings and hire a PR man,' I said.

He nodded. 'You've hit the nail on the flat bit, Albert, my boy.'

'I don't have anything very promising.'

'I'm considering all offers.'

'I wanted you to check out what's in the files on a man called Lance Whisstock.' I spelled it for him.

He frowned.

'What's wrong?'

'I've heard the name somewhere.'

'So much the better,' I said.

'O.K.,' he said. 'You got it. Anything else?'

'I have another job that started with a fake birth certificate.'

'Why the hell does someone fake a birth certificate? To pretend the kid is legitimate?'

'I don't know yet. But there must have been something wrong with the real one.'

Miller blinked. 'If not baby-snatching then maybe baby sale,' he said. He sucked on his candy cane. 'What can I do to help?'

It was December, but an offer like that is Christmas any time of year for a humble private detective.

FIVE

The Murchisons' former home was on the south side of New York Street, past the Indiana Women's Reformatory. I found a large, three-floor wooden building at the address, with a big open porch. There was an air of neglect about the place. Patches of mud among grass and weed stalks. A snowfall of flaked paint. The steps gave an inch under my weight and I've been on a diet. As I approached the front door I saw a couple of holes clean through the portico roof.

A mounted metal display unit had places for six name-cards next to push buttons on the outside wall beside the door. But in only one was there a slip of paper. Two others had pencil scrawls written in the spaces. Perhaps there were vacancies.

I tried the button next to the carded name.

I heard the attached bell ring close by. A young man in a T-shirt which only partly covered multi-coloured tattoos on both arms appeared at the door.

'Hello,' he said, as brightly as his surroundings were depressing. 'Come on in.'

I entered the hallway, and we stood outside his open door at the foot of the stairs.

'What can I do for you?'

I said, 'I am looking for the owner, or somebody who could tell me about some people who used to live in this building.'

'Jeez,' he said and chewed on his lower lip. 'How long ago was the people living here?'

'Quite a while,' I said. 'Late thirties, early forties.'

He looked as if he couldn't believe what he had heard. 'Thirties as in nineteen thirties?'

'The very same.'

He gave up. 'I don't know nobody from that old.'

'Can you tell me where to find the owner?'

'I don't know who owns the place, except he never puts a face in around here. There's quite a few things that ought to be done,' he said earnestly.

'But you pay rent?'

'Oh yeah. Sure do.' He stepped past me, back to the porch, and pointed down New York to the east. 'See that junk store near the corner?'

I looked. 'Next to the drug store?'

'I pay in there to a guy called Dwayne. But I don't know anything about the owner. I've been here about as long as anybody and I've never seen him.'

'How long have you been in residence?'

'Nearly a year.'

In 'Quality Second Hand Goods' a man in his early thirties dozed with his feet up on a quality second-hand table. My entry triggered a bell and he twitched as he awoke.

He looked at me a full five seconds before he saw me. It was as if he wasn't used to having his business day disturbed by a customer.

I could sympathise with the feeling.

Shaking his head to clear it, he proceeded to shake other bits of anatomy, working his way down. Then he stood and greeted me with a shambling grin. 'Just lookin'?'

Nothing quite like the hard sell.

'A guy in a house across the road says he pays his rent to you,' I said.

38

Dwayne scratched the top of his head and I was fearful he was going to go through the dance of the seven veins again. 'Yeah,' he agreed. 'I do a little collecting. What you want, an apartment?' He scratched some more. 'I think there's one or two empty over there. I don't quite remember how many there are altogether, but I can get the keys and look.'

'No, I'm not looking for an apartment,' I said.

'Oh.'

'I'm trying to find someone who knows about the place. From the old days. I'm trying to find out about some people who used to live there. I thought maybe the owner could help.'

'Possible,' Dwayne said. 'Charlie's a pretty together guy.'

'Can I have his name and address?'

Dwayne shrugged. 'He's just Charlie to me. He comes in on Monday to pick up his bread. Tenants are supposed to drop it off here Friday night, but some of them are always late. Gives me the weekend to go and take it off them before Charlie comes by. Big guy, Charlie. They don't usually mess us around.'

'You don't know his full name?'

'Charlie. He's sort of, well, known around the neighbourhood. Came along a few years ago, asked me if I'd do his collecting. I get a percent. It's small but it's steady.'

'Is there anybody you could direct me to who's been here for a long time?'

'How long?'

'Since the thirties or forties?'

'That would make them pretty old,' he noted. 'I've been here about as long as anybody.'

'How long is that?'

'Since I was a kid,' Dwayne said. 'This was my dad's place, till he left.'

'And has that house always been apartments?'

39

He was about to say that it had when the question jogged a cog in his memory. 'You know I haven't thought about it for years, but I'm damned if it didn't used to be a cat house. When I was a kid. My dad did odd jobs over there and I wasn't supposed to know what went on, but I did. Then somebody must of forgot to pay somebody and the cops came in and closed it down. Damn, the things you forget about.' He began to twitch again.

From the public phone in the drugstore next door I put Miller on to tracking down the police records for the action taken in the late fifties or early sixties which was as close as Dwayne could fix it. Then I walked circuitously back to my car, looking at the neighbourhood. The women's prison didn't exactly give it class, but there was a nice view of the city from Highland Park. And clearly the area, like the New York Street house, had seen more vital and prosperous days.

I decided to make a little visit to The Fandango bar, though the major effort to find grandson Whisstock would wait until I had what background research information was available. I went to Illinois Street, but by way of another address in my notebook. The other former Murchison home, on 42nd Street.

I made a slow drive-past and saw a compact and conventional one-storey brick house in a small plot of ground. I didn't get anything worth a notebook entry and left it at that.

The Fandango was small and the air was murky with stale tobacco smoke even though none of the three men at the bar were smoking. There was nothing notable – or Spanish – about the decor.

I sat at the counter away from the other men. As I did so, one of them rose from his stool and passed through a gap to

40

take pride of place behind the bar.

'Beer,' I said.

He drew it and put the glass in front of me. I gave him a five and he counted the change out for me slowly and carefully in front of me. I left it where it lay.

'Get a lot of guys complaining about the change?' I asked.

He shrugged with a little smile. 'Like to avoid what trouble I can.'

I nodded. I downed the beer quickly and asked for another.

When it came the barman took the price off my pile. I said to him, 'I haven't been in here before.'

'I know,' he said.

'Somebody told me I might come across a friend of mine here.'

'Oh yeah?'

'Guy named Lance. You know him?'

'We get a lot of Lances in here,' he said.

'Stocky guy, mid-twenties. Long dark hair, beard.'

'We get a lot of guys in their mid-twenties with long dark hair and beards.'

'Ah,' I said.

I took a drink of my beer and said, 'To tell you the truth I've never met this friend of mine.'

'Is that a fact.'

'But I was told that he might be able to help me out.'

'In that case I hope you find him,' the barman said.

'I'm not a cop,' I said.

'Go on!'

I took out my ID and laid it on the bar. 'I'm a private detective.'

The man studied my documentation. 'O.K., son. I'll accept that you are over twenty-one.' He raised his eyes to mine.

I said, 'No fuss. No bother. He may be able to help me and if he can there will be something in it for him.'

I downed the rest of my beer, gathered my cash and left.

It was after three-thirty when I crossed my threshold again. While I was out, there had been a phone call. Before listening to the message, I hung my coat in the closet.

The telephone rang.

I picked up the receiver and cut in over the machine as it was saying, 'Albert Samson is not in his office.'

'Yes he is,' I said.

'Make your mind up,' Miller said.

I switched off the tape.

'I just came in.'

'What do you want me to do about it?'

'You don't sound very happy with life,' I said. 'What's the matter?'

'Nothing. Everything. What should be the matter? You want such dope as I have on your requests for assistance or not?'

'Dope doesn't mean "information" these days, lieutenant. Be careful how you speak. Somebody might be listening.'

'I'll give you your vice raid first. All right?'

'Sure.'

He read out the names of six women, none familiar to me.

'What charges?'

'Prostitution.'

'Only the troops? No officers?'

'There's nothing on record.'

'Would that mean somebody influential intervened?'

'Probably only that some money found the right out-stretched palm. Not that things work that way these days.'

'Is there any indication who owned the building? Or

42

about who really operated the business?'

'I've got nothing here. And I don't recognise the names of any of the arresting officers as current.'

'It was a long time ago.'

'I was on the force then,' he said.

I let it pass.

'Which brings me nicely to Lance Whisstock.'

'O.K.,' I said.

'He has no record of any kind. Not even a speeding citation.'

'Oh.'

'But I placed the name.'

I waited. Finally I said, 'And?'

'He's a cop, Al. One of my estimable colleagues. College boy. A sergeant.'

'The hell he is!'

We shared a silence.

This time Miller broke it. He asked slowly, 'What is your interest in him?'

'At this point I don't know,' I said.

'You have a client with an interest?'

'I have a client who told me Lance's grandad says Lance is mixing in bad company.'

'Whisstock is undercover so that's not surprising.'

'Undercover?' The surprise inevitably showed in my voice.

'He's a narc,' Miller said. Then sternly, 'You know better than to put him at risk with this information.'

'Yes.'

'And for the record grandpa is Captain Warren Foley, retired.'

'Captain, as in . . .'

'Indianapolis Police Department.'

'I see,' I said. Which was a lie.

'I think you might have a question or two for your client,

Al.'

'I think you're right,' I said.

'And Albert, keep me informed.'

I almost passed on the message on the answering machine, assuming that it had been from Miller. But then I thought again and gave it a play.

'Oh, a recording,' a male voice said. 'I'll be brief then. In a nutshell, I am the long-lost Lindbergh baby. I have evidence. If you help me prove who I am, you can have 50 per cent of the profits from the story and a share of the estate. Call me between seven-fifteen and seven-fifty tonight.'

He left a number. I didn't make a note of it. After all, what do you find in a nutshell?

I decided to sit for a while, to try to sort out the day's results. On both cases. I retreated to my desk.

In the inner office.

As advertised on television.

I began to work through my activities, making complete notes, ultimately for use in the reports I would make to my clients.

I got as far as the Murchisons' first house. The big one. The brothel.

After a few minutes sitting, pen in hand, over that unfinished page, I got up, put on my coat and went out.

With a certain awareness of irony, I parked my van in the lot which now stands on the site of the first office building I operated from as a P.I. And it was ten to five by the time I got myself through the door at the Marion County Birth Certificates Office.

With a deep sigh a tall man with a bushy red moustache approached the inquiry counter. 'You want to know the way to somewhere else, right?' he asked.

'I want some information about a birth,' I said.

He looked at his watch. He shook his head. He sighed again. 'I've been here all day long. Half of it sitting on my hands. Now, ten minutes before I'm due to go home, have a shower, go out to dinner, see a movie and get laid, you come in. What's wrong with nine in the morning? Or even three in the afternoon? Jesus! I can tell by looking that you want action now. Tomorrow ain't good enough. Am I right? Jesus!'

'Can you tell by looking at me that there's twenty bucks in it for you?'

He took a second look. 'Maybe I can do without the movie.'

The notion was simple enough. The names on Mrs Douglas Belter's birth certificate were wrong, but maybe the date and place of birth were right.

The twenty-dollar investment was for a list of the details of all females born in Marion County on February 5, 1936.

Whether it would produce anything depended on the reason the names were changed on the phony certificate.

I had a scenario, based on my discovery of the kind of business which had been operating in the New York Street house fifteen years after Ella Murchison had moved out of it. Suppose the brothel was a venerable establishment, founded in the thirties. Suppose it had been run by Big Ma Murchison and her old man, Big Pa. Suppose one of the 'girls' got pregnant. Girls do. Suppose, for some reason, Big Ma had decided to take the child on.

It seemed worth a shot. At least it included a reason for obscuring the background of a child.

My moustached clerk earned his twenty.

He found it under 'W'. A girl of six pounds and nine ounces had been born that day to 'Miss Daisy Wines'. No

45

father listed. The child was named Paula Helen Wines. The mother's address was that of the Murchisons' house on New York Street.

SIX

With a photocopy of the Paula Wines birth certificate in my pocket, I drove home.

I felt a degree of satisfaction because I'd learned something directly from having deduced the right question to ask.

There had been two more phone calls while I was out. I rewound the tape and had a listen.

The first was from Tanya Wilkerson.

Tanya!

She said, 'Thanks for the note. I don't think my director is interested in your experiences, but I'll pass the idea on to him. Maybe I shouldn't say this, but what little mail we've had about the piece on you seemed to think the item was a gag and you were an actor. Might you consider a new career? Ha ha.'

She shouldn't have said it.

The second call was from Douglas A. Belter. He said, 'I've been worried all day about the best thing to do. Paula is supposed to be making those notes for you, but if you were to come to the house at seven, you could ask her directly anything that might fill . . .'

The message finished there, because he'd overrun the space on the tape. He had been speaking slowly and hesitating over words. I felt sorry for the man.

Belter's evident distress took the shine off my self-congratulations. There is a game-playing side to my work which provides occasional pleasures. But in the end I am dealing with things that have painful meanings to the people involved.

My self-examination was interrupted when my landlord, Albert Connah, parked his Caddy out front. He came in and demanded beer.

The premises my office-home is a part of used to be a lumber yard. Albert uses the storage bays to keep a huge stock of glass. He thinks the price will rise sharply with the cost of energy. I pay no rent, and in exchange I keep an eye on his property. There is an unwritten side to our contract which gives him access to my beer stock. We also keep a basketball and shoot some hoops occasionally in a basket mounted out back – well away from the glass.

'Hey,' he said, 'I stopped by 'cause I wondered if you wanted a ticket to the Pacers tonight. Or are you already going?'

The Indianapolis pro basketball team. Glass Albert is a fan. I have a mild interest.

'Working tonight,' I said. 'Sorry. Thanks.'

'Working,' he said, pushing the top of his nose up with a finger to suggest the word had an unwholesome odour. 'Since when?'

He drained the beer and left.

I arrived outside the Belter house at four minutes before seven. The place, on Meridian Hills Boulevard just south of 73rd Street, was spectacular, and reminded me of my daughter's postcards from Alpine ski lodges. Vast porches and huge windows underneath steeply angled roofs, the whole wooden structure perched on supports which raised and levelled it above a gentle slope. It was too dark to see what sort of kingdom it surveyed, but when I'd looked it up on my map before setting out, it had seemed likely to overlook the Meridian Hills Country Club's golf course.

Sitting in my van in the driveway I felt extraordinarily out of place. I took my notebook and went to the front door.

Before I could ring the bell the door was opened by a pale petite elderly Oriental woman with hazel eyes and black hair.

'I'm Albert Samson,' I said. 'I have an appointment with Mr and Mrs Belter.'

'We're expecting you, Mr Samson,' she said. 'Would you come with me, please?'

Her voice bore no accent other than a mild Hoosier one.

She led me to a room which, though at the back of the house, appeared to be the main living-room. It was as big as my entire office and living quarters. On two sides ceiling-to-floor drapes provided undulating walls. A massive open-sided fireplace hived off about one-third of the space to give semi-isolation to an enormous dining table. There was a substantial glowing wood fire.

Douglas Belter, in suit and tie, approached me from the far side of the room as the woman who had to be the housekeeper Tamae and I entered. About six feet from me he stopped. 'Thank you for coming,' he said.

'No problem.'

He half-pivoted to lead my attention back to the area of the room he'd just come from, and there a light and lithe woman, who looked younger than the forty-six I knew her to be, rose from one of a half-dozen deep chairs. She had sandy hair which was short and in tight little curls. Her dress was black and plain.

'How *do* you do, Mr Samson?' she said. She extended her hand and shook mine warmly. 'I'm Paula Belter. What a bit of a mess, eh?' She smiled briefly and turned to her husband. 'Perhaps you'd get Mr Samson a drink, Doug. I don't know about him, but I'm so keyed up I wouldn't say no myself.'

'Of course,' Belter said. 'What would you like, dear?'

'A gentle g and t, I think,' she said.

Belter looked at me.

'Beer, thanks.'

'Tamae?'

'A Bloody Mary please, Mr Belter.'

Belter disappeared behind the fire. The rest of us settled in the cluster of chairs, which encircled a coffee table made from a polished cross-section of a tree trunk.

The other major piece of furniture in the room was a grand piano which was well away from the drapes and centred on an oval deep-pile rug.

Belter brought the drinks on a tray and served them from the table.

It was the first time I'd ever drunk beer from cut glass.

I became more relaxed.

Paula Belter downed most of her beverage in one go. 'Well,' she said. 'Bite the bullet time.'

'I think –' her husband began.

Mrs Belter interrupted him without hesitation. 'Doug said that you wanted me to make a list of facts from my childhood, and I tried,' she said. 'But as a request, it seemed vague and likely I would put down a lot of things that you didn't want to know. So it seemed better to let you ask more directly for the information you want.'

Belter looked uneasy and Tamae sat still with her red drink perched on a knee.

The three of them watched me closely. I said, 'What I intended was information which might help me place your family, as close to the time you were born as possible. When the starting point is a false document, with misleading "facts" . . .' I stopped as they all grew visibly more tense. My eyes flicked from one to another before I soldiered on.

'It is difficult to know how best to reconstruct the details you want established.'

No one said anything.

'But,' I said, 'I've had a little luck and I think I can tell you things you don't already know.'

I explained briefly what I had done during the day, calling on Mrs Murchison, getting addresses from telephone books and then taking a chance on a short cut.

'The result is that I have found a birth certificate for a girl, born the same date as on the false certificate. It gives Mrs Murchison's as the home address, and the child's first and middle names are Paula and Helen.'

I took the birth certificate copy from my pocket and passed it across the table towards Mrs Belter.

'I have no conclusive proof yet that this is your real birth certificate but it seems a pretty good bet. And, of course, it proves nothing about the origin of the other one.'

All three of them made slight movements to take the paper, but Douglas Belter and Tamae acceded to Mrs Belter's natural right to be first.

She took up the copy and read it through, blinking several times. She read it again.

Then she put it gently on the table and leaned back in her chair. She folded her hands in her lap and looked at me. As her husband took the document, she said quietly, 'So you think that I am Paula Helen Wines.'

'It seems very possible to me,' I said.

'Good heavens,' she said. She breathed deeply. 'Who would ever have thought that deciding to go on a little trip would mean I suddenly became a whole new person.' She changed the position of her hands. Then seeming not to be able to settle, she rubbed and wrung them. 'What a thing to happen,' she said loudly. 'Nearly fifty years old and . . .'

The agitation spiralled and she stood up. Immediately Belter too rose and moved to her.

'It's like a cliff crumbling,' Paula Belter said. 'And I'm falling.'

Belter didn't speak, but he led her out of the room.

Tamae and I watched them leave.

Then Tamae tilted forward and took the sheet of paper from the table top. She read it quickly, and put it down. She stared at me for several seconds. She said, 'I am Tamae Mitsuki.'

'Hello,' I said. I offered my hand.

She hesitated before she shook it as lightly as a butterfly kiss.

'I am the housekeeper and I helped Mrs Belter bring up the two boys.'

'Mr Belter said that you were one of the family.'

'I hope so.'

'Is Mrs Belter all right?'

'Oh yes. She'll be back before you leave and you won't know there was anything wrong. She will lie down for two minutes and then it will be O.K.'

'Good,' I said genuinely.

'She'll realise that she is the same person and has the same life. She'll think of the boys.'

'Of course.' Then I said, 'I don't know whether I could have presented it in a less startling way.'

Tamae shrugged lightly.

Douglas Belter returned to the room but didn't sit again. 'She'll be better in a bit,' he said.

I nodded. I said, 'This doesn't automatically solve your initial problem, but it should give you a good start.'

He seemed uncertain. 'Which problem was that?'

'Getting a passport for your trip. Your lawyer will be able to find out what procedures need taking care of, once you've confirmed the identity.'

'Yes . . .' he said, without absorbing. 'And how does one go about that?'

'I haven't had a chance to look into it,' I said. 'But I'm sure that you need a little time to get your bearings. Meanwhile I'll make a formal report on what I've done, cost the time, and by then you'll know if there's anything else you want me to do.'

'All right,' Belter said vacantly.

I rose to go. And wondered whether the turmoil might have longer-term effects on the husband than on the wife.

We made our way to the front door.

But as I was about to leave, a rush of footsteps caught all our attentions.

Paula Belter, half wrapped in a silk kimono dressing gown, burst around a corner. 'You're not going!' she said.

'I thought . . .'

'I want you to find her,' she said.

'Find . . . ?'

'This . . . this Daisy Wines. I want you to find my mother.'

SEVEN

Before I left it was arranged that Douglas Belter would come to my office in the morning.

He arrived just before ten. I was sitting at the old upright piano, poking at it with my typing finger. I had prepared Belter's report after breakfast. It hadn't taken long, so I was giving the digit a little extra exercise, to try to keep it supple.

Belter stood inside the door as if stunned when he found me playing. And I've never had a lesson.

I stopped and greeted him. He appeared serious and clean, as he had each time I'd met him, but now, with his wife's developing history, there was an odd look about him too. I wondered whether he had anywhere to go to relax, any friend to turn to.

We went to my inner office.

'What Paula said last night,' he began quickly, 'about finding her mother, that holds.'

'All right. I'll give it a try.'

'I thought,' he said, 'that we could establish what course of action would be the best to follow.'

'I promised you a report and reckoning to date and you might look that over first,' I said. From the central drawer of my desk I passed him two sheets of paper.

He took the document, but dismissed the idea of reading it. 'Thank you, thank you. But can we get on?'

'You realise, I'm sure, that the most efficient way to get the facts you want is from Mrs Murchison. And that your wife and yourself are both better placed than I am to go to her and say, look, we know now, so tell us about it.'

'We saw her this morning,' he said simply. He shook his head. 'The nurses said she was all right, but we didn't get two words of sense.'   .

I said, 'Then there are two or three ways I can try to trace Daisy Wines but there is no guarantee that I can get a lead on her, any more than it is certain she is still alive.'

'Of course.'

'But you should consider something else.'

He looked at me.

'What I find might not be pleasant to know.'

'What do you mean?'

'Let's assume, as now seems likely, that Daisy Wines is your wife's mother. Then she gave her child away. That needn't be an irresponsible act, but it certainly might be. She might have been an irresponsible or disreputable person.'

Belter studied my face and asked, perceptively, 'Do you know something you haven't told me?'

'Only,' I said, 'that the house at the address on the birth certificate was being used as a brothel in the late 1950s. It's in the report. I know of no direct connection back to the time Daisy Wines and Mrs Murchison lived there. But it opens the possibility, by association, that I might find out that Daisy Wines was a prostitute. Are you prepared for something like that?'

'I am,' Belter said darkly, 'I want to know what is what. And you need spare no expense which will expedite this knowledge.'

'I think those instructions are pretty clear,' I said.

I sat for a few moments after he left trying to remember if

I'd ever heard the phrase 'spare no expense' used in real life before.

I went to work. I drove into town and parked in the Arena lot. I crossed to the City-County Building, but instead of entering the Police Department wing, I went to the judicial side which also houses the city and county records offices. There I 'arranged' for one of the clerks to find the ownership history of the New York Street house for me, quickly. I spared no expense.

From the records office I made the short trip to Birth Certificates in Ohio.

My moustachioed friend had bags under his eyes. But he smiled at me and was content.

'What can I do for you?'

What he could do was search for Daisy Wines' birth certificate. It was possible she'd been born in Marion County. Maybe I was having a run of luck.

Then I went to see Miller.

'You still look awful,' I said, 'but I won't tell you because it will probably only get you down.'

'I appreciate that.'

I thought about asking how his family was, but decided that too would be depressing.

I said, 'You invited me to come in if I had things that I wanted done.'

'Yeah, yeah.'

'I'm trying to trace a woman and all I know about her is her name and the date she had a child.'

Miller scrutinised me.

'I want you to have some things checked out. All right?'

'Like what?'

'Whether she ever died, whether she has hospital records anywhere, whether the child was adopted legally, whether she has a criminal record.'

'Child, huh?' he said.

I shrugged.

'O.K. Give me the name and stuff. What have I got to lose?'

I felt sorry for the man.

On my way out I walked through the central foyer back to the judicial side of the building. I hoped my commissioned history of the New York Street address had been completed.

And it had. Life was a smooth downhill roll.

The building had had five owners since 1921. The title changed in 1938, 1940, 1945, and in 1972. The owners were Samuel H. Garrison, G. Bennett R. Edwards, Mrs G. Bennett R. Edwards, Michael P. Carson, and Edward C. Carson.

My bet was that the 'C' stood for Charlie.

The Daisy Wines search was certain to take longer so I got my van and headed west of north, to Biarritz House.

I didn't recognise the woman at the desk in the foyer and she didn't notice me until I cleared my throat in front of her. I explained that I wanted a word with Mrs Howard about Ella Murchison.

'Ella Murchison,' the woman repeated, with her eyebrows raised.

I smiled and asked, 'Why do you say it like that?'

'Every other person who comes in wants to see Ella. Has she come into money or something?'

'Life has made you a cynic, ma'am,' I said.

'Not life. Buzz Gordon, my husband. Connie Howard is probably upstairs. Shall I call her for you?'

'If you would, please.'

The bustling Mrs Howard came down the building's open curving staircase four minutes later. She nodded as she approached me.

'You were here a day or two ago, weren't you?'

'Yesterday,' I said.

'Ella Murchison,' she said.

'That's right.' I gave her my name again.

'What's going on, Mr Samson?' she asked. 'You're back here. Her daughter and son-in-law visited early this morning. The daughter's housekeeper is in there now.' She flipped her hands apart for a moment, a kind of manual question mark.

'They think that Mrs Murchison might be able to remember a woman they would like to trace, a long-lost member of the family they only heard about recently. I suppose people are coming in shifts because of her reputation for intermittent lucidity and they would like someone with her if she does become more communicative again.'

Mrs Howard was not happy. 'I know I said that she has these incoherent times . . . But it's not like a faucet, on for a while and then off. She's liable to worry about these poisons any time, but for the most part I find you can talk to her perfectly well. Compared to the general standard of our residents, she is very aware.'

'Yesterday I found that she wouldn't stick to the subject. At least not my subject.'

'Maybe that was because she doesn't know you very well.'

'Before yesterday, not at all.'

'Perhaps she's just not used to people coming through at quite such a rate.'

To underline the point, Tamae Mitsuki passed from Mrs Murchison's corridor into the foyer.

She saw me as I saw her and did not seem surprised. I excused myself, but Mrs Howard followed me as I approached the housekeeper.

I said, 'Hello.'

'Hello, Mr Samson.'

58

'How is Mrs Murchison today?'

'She seems real low. I'm afraid that I couldn't get through to her at all.'

I nodded understandingly.

Mrs Howard shook her head as if not understanding.

We must have made quite a double act.

Connie Howard said, 'She took her breakfast without any fuss and we talked about the weather.'

'That's what she talked to me about,' Mrs Mitsuki said. 'The weather. Poor lady.'

'Have you known her long?' I asked.

'Oh, yes. Years and years. I came to Indianapolis after the war with my son, and Mrs Murchison rented us a room and later gave me a job. Despite the prejudice against the Japanese in those days. We were very grateful.'

'Where did you come here from?'

'California. My husband died in internment. I wanted to get away.'

'How did you pick Indianapolis?'

'I can hardly remember,' she said with a small smile. 'I had heard the name and I liked its sound. I thought that someplace that remembered its Indian origins might be an easier place for my son and me to fit in.'

'I wish I could believe that your expectations were fulfilled,' I said.

'It's worked out O.K.,' she said philosophically.

'Is your son still in the city?'

'Oh yes. He runs a restaurant.'

'Which one?'

'It's called The Rising Sun. On Northwestern Avenue a few miles north of I-465.'

'I'll have to try it one day.'

She smiled delicately. 'I have to go now,' she said.

'Nice to see you again.'

She left.

59

I turned to Mrs Howard, who was still by my side. 'I'm sorry to have kept you from what you were doing.'

'You're not,' she said, looking after Mrs Mitsuki. 'I would have gone if I wanted to.'

'I didn't really come to see Mrs Murchison,' I said. 'I came to get an idea from someone who knows her well as to whether we're likely to get the information we want from her.'

'I know Ella better than anybody else,' Connie Howard said. 'I'm surprised she hasn't helped you already, unless, perhaps, this "information" is something she wouldn't want to think about.'

'There might be some unpleasantness associated with it,' I said.

'I see.'

'Mrs Howard, we would be grateful for any help.' I gave her my card. 'I'm employed by Mr Douglas Belter.'

'Yes?' she said.

'Mr Belter hopes to trace this relative, a woman named Daisy Wines. He would gladly offer some money either to you or a charity you might nominate if it is possible for you to expedite matters.'

Sternly, Mrs Howard said, 'You may tell Mr Belter that I am not available for hire to hound old women.'

'I hope that is not what I was suggesting, Mrs Howard.'

'It certainly sounded like it to me, Mr Samson.'

And when I thought about it, it sounded like it to me too. I felt about five centimetres high.

I licked my wounds in a telephone booth, getting and then trying the number of Edward C. Carson.

The woman who answered said, 'He ain't here, mister. And I don't know when he's coming back.'

'Is there somewhere I might have a chance of catching him?'

'Catching him?'

'To talk to,' I said.

'I don't know,' she said again. 'He could be anywhere during the day. Charlie really gets around, you know? But at nights he'll be at the club, of course.'

'Club?'

'Sure. Aren't you another singer or something?'

'No.'

'Oh. I thought you was.'

'Which club would that be?'

'Rovers Lounge. You know it?'

'No.'

'Out English Avenue, near Christian Park.'

'I'll find it. And he's there every night?'

'Yeah. Don't like nobody else counting his money, Charlie.'

Then I made my other call. To Normal Bates.

He answered almost immediately.

'This is Albert Samson, Mr Bates.'

'Ah,' he said. 'The redoubtable detective. What can I do for you?'

'I would like to stop by.'

He paused. In my mind he was noting that I hadn't said why I wanted to see him.

'When do you want to come?' he asked.

'How about now?'

'All right. I look forward to hearing what you have to say.' He hung up.

I was about twenty minutes from Tarkington Tower. I was also hungry. I considered stopping at a fast foodery on the way. But in the end I didn't. I feel I'm a little bit sharper when the tank is low.

Bates sported yellow braces this time, and he shook my hand firmly at the door. He waved me in and allowed me to

61

lead us to his sitting room. He sat in his chair but the straight chair from the computer had been moved into place for me.

He faced me with his gleaming eyes. 'I suspect you have learned something,' he said.

I nodded. 'You're right.'

'Let's have it.'

'I've learned that Lance Whisstock is a police sergeant on undercover assignment,' I said. 'As you well know.'

'Yes,' Bates said without surprise. 'A rising star over there. If he has the luck not to get killed, he'll have an illustrious career.'

'Captain Foley must be very proud of his grandson,' I said.

Bates' eyes twinkled. 'Good, Mr Samson. Good.'

I began to speak, but Bates raised a hand to stop me. 'I know, I know. You are not amused that I hire you to find out things I already know.'

'I don't take it for a joke, Mr Bates. But I don't understand what you're up to.'

'How else am I to get an idea of whether you are any good?' Instead of waiting for an answer, however, he swivelled his chair to face his panoramic window.

I waited.

'It's a fascinating place, Indianapolis,' he said finally.

Not everybody's view, but I said nothing.

'In its way a sampler of the history of the whole country over the last hundred and fifty years. Growth. Migrants making their fortunes. Here, in meat packing, breweries, banking, bakeries. It was an important place before the war, you know.'

'Yes?'

'Broadway shows came before they went to New York. Top music people. You ever heard of Paderewski?'

He was a Polish pianist and politician. 'No,' I said.

'Long hair. Threw it around a lot at the piano.'

'Oh,' I said.

'I want you to do another job for me,' he said. He turned his chair to me again.

'What this time? To see if I can find out which president cut down a cherry tree and couldn't tell a lie?'

His eyes fixed mine and he wasn't smiling. 'This job is real, serious and large. It will mean regular work for you over an extended period of time and I will give you a substantial retainer. It involves nothing illegal or dangerous. It starts immediately. You've got to be interested.'

He was right. I had to be interested.

'How soon is immediately?' I asked.

'Tomorrow. Or even today.'

'I am committed to another case at the moment.'

'A case as important or lucrative as what I am offering you?'

'No. But I have agreed to take it,' I said.

'I see.' Bates said. 'Something interesting?'

'A family wishes to locate a woman but can give me no information more current than 1936.'

'How do you go about a problem like that?'

'I try to find someone who knew her. I check for anything that might have been recorded somewhere.'

'It sounds a formidable task.'

'People leave their mark. I just hope this woman's was adequately indelible.'

'It does not sound like something you will be able to wrap up quickly,' he said.

'Probably not,' I agreed.

'And you can't get out of it?'

'That's not how I go about things, Mr Bates. But tell me more about what you want me to do. It is possible that I could get started, or get someone else to get started, and then pick it up full-time when this case is completed.'

'The first part involves your talking to people in Boston. There is no way you can go about it other than whole-heartedly.'

'Then I'm sorry,' I said.

And the more I thought about it, the sorrier I was. Full employment is the same kind of dreamland for a private detective as it is for a country.

'I am an old man, Mr Samson. And being old is not simple. There *are* advantages. For one, an old man does not have to sacrifice the present for rewards in later life. For another you know who your real friends are. But the disadvantages are terrible. They lie in the decline of your power, both over your own mind and body, and over events which affect you and your friends. Do you understand what I'm saying?'

'Not fully.'

For a few seconds he was silent again. 'You are still young, although perhaps you don't appreciate it because you are older than you have ever been. But, my God, what I could do if I were your age!'

I didn't know what to say.

'So, even if I offer you a guaranteed term of employment lasting for, say, six months, or a year, you would not be willing to work for me exclusively beginning immediately.'

'Give me a little time. I'll see what kind of accommodation I can make.'

'Time I am short of,' he said with a sigh. We waited again, while he thought. 'Suppose you let me know as soon as you can, and I'll decide then whether it is too late or not.'

'All right,' I said.

Our meeting was at an end. Bates turned his chair and his attention back to the city which spread out below him. I

64

rose and left and walked down the eleven flights of stairs trying to guess what kind of year-long job couldn't wait a few days to be commenced.

EIGHT

I remembered I was hungry as I left Tarkington Towers.
But instead of diving into the nearest pizza parlour for a
sandwich, I called my woman to invite her out for lunch.

If I could wait three-quarters of an hour, she could make
it.

I took my mind off food by visiting the Birth Certificates
office.

I was greeted as a friend.

'I don't know how old you figure this lady might have
been, but I've been back through 1900 so far and there's no
entry for a Daisy Wines.'

I thought about it. It would make her older than thirty-
five when she had her child.

'Can you go back farther?' I asked.

'Sure.'

'1890?'

He smiled broadly. Windfalls probably always made him
grin.

'I'll call you later this afternoon,' I said.

I've just been offered six months' continuous work,' I said.

'Good heavens!' My lady friend was impressed.

'Or maybe a year.'

'Doing what?'

'I'm not quite sure.'

She studied the menu. Not that there is much to choose from lunchtime at Joe's Fine Food. 'I gather from your vagueness that you have declined six months' continuous work.'

'Nope. I'd take it like a shot.'

'What's the problem?'

'He wants me to start full time today. Tomorrow at the latest. But I am committed to another case.'

She studied me. Knowledgeable enough to ask, as Bates had, whether I could farm it out to someone else, and knowledgeable enough to know the answer was that I wouldn't.

'I can tell when you are working on something unusual,' she said. 'You get this air of sad preoccupation.'

'I'm trying to find a woman named Daisy Wines.'

'What kind of name is that?'

'If I knew, I'd be that much closer.'

'Perhaps one of the French Wines?'

Mail and a telephone call had arrived while I was out. I went for the white envelope among the brown. List of wedding guests at the Belters' wedding.

None of the names meant anything to me.

Then I sorted through the four new bills before listening to the message on my answering machine.

If there'd been four calls and one bill I'd have been a lot happier.

The single message was, 'Hi. I'm Wendy Winslow and I work for CCC, the Champaign Cable Company based in Champaign, Illinois, the bubbly city. We've got an Indianapolis franchise now and when we saw you on TV we wondered if you might be interested in a regular spot as a TV private eye, helping our viewers and making reports on your cases. Can we talk about it?' She left a telephone number.

You can get a lot of message on tape if you're a fast talker.

I played it again and sat for quite a while wondering if there was any chance at all that this wasn't some kind of joke.

At a quarter past four Miller called.

'Why is it,' he asked, 'that when I need a boost all you give me is junk to do?'

'Are you telling me something, officer?'

'I'm telling you that I have drawn a blank, blank, blank and blank on adoption, hospital, death and arrest records for a Daisy Wines. I also had the voting register, social security and the IRS check for her.'

'Very good,' I said. 'I'm impressed.'

'And I drew more blanks. Seems like you're looking for a healthy, law-abiding living lady without a sense of civic duty, who has never held a job or earned more than four hundred bucks in any one year. There can't be many around like that in *this* city.'

Which left me depressed by the rather simpler explanation that Daisy Wines had not remained in this city. Not, however, the time to mention this possibility to Miller.

'How old is this broad supposed to be?' he continued.

'She had a child in 1936.'

'Mmmm. So, she was at least what at the time? Ten?'

'I think we can safely assume she was a little older than that. Why?'

'If she qualified she might have applied for Medicaid or some other age benefit somewhere. Just a thought.'

He hung up to work on it.

I called Birth Certificates. My moustached buddy reported that he had been unable to find any record of Daisy Wines' birth any time since 1885.

A lot of doors marked 'maybe' were closing quickly.

I called Miller back.

'Oh,' he said.

'Show more enthusiasm,' I said. 'It means I'm trying hard for you.'

'Make it quick, Al. I'm planning to throw myself under a train and it leaves Union Station in six minutes.'

'I want to know any arrest records on Samuel H. Garrison, G. Bennett R. Edwards, Mrs G. Bennett R. Edwards, Michael P. Carson and Edward C. Carson.'

'Just who might these distinguished members of the social register be?'

'Past and present owners of a house where Daisy Wines once lived. And can I have these quickly, Jerry? I'm going out to meet one of them tonight and if there's something to know, I'd like to know it.'

'You're lucky to live in the computer age,' he said.

While the silicon chips were pulsating, I thumbed through the phone book. Of past New York Street owners, only an Edward C. Carson had a current listing.

Miller called back in less than half an hour.

'Don't tell me,' I said. 'More blanks.'

'Some live rounds this time, for what they're worth.'

'Shoot.'

'The interesting ones first, eh? For instance, George Bennett Raymond Edwards. He was shot to death in his own home on April 21st, 1940.'

'Well, well.'

'And the delightful Mrs Edwards was tried for his murder in July 1940. But she got off.'

'You say he was shot in his home. That was the New York Street house?'

'No, no. On North Meridian. I deal only in high-class stuff. I have the address. You want it?'

Sombrely I said, 'I want it.'

69

After he read it out to me, he said, 'These were big money people, Al. It's got all the signs of a big scandal case at the time.'

'It says that in your computer, does it?'

'It says there are newspaper reports in the paper file, that the victim was the Bennett heir, whatever that was, and that he had half a dozen drunk arrests but no convictions. Sounds like playboy time to me. Stands to reason.'

'Can I have a copy of what you've got?'

'As long as you don't show it to anyone, pick it up yourself, and say thank you.'

'Thank you. What else is there?'

'A bad cheque arrest and conviction on Samuel H. Garrison. Michael P. Carson is now deceased. Edward C. Carson is his son. Michael Carson ran a few clubs through the thirties and forties. He had some gaming convictions and an assault arrest. The suggestion was that by the end of the forties he was mostly on the wrong side of the fast buck tracks. But there are no arrests after '43 and he was never a very big hood. He was questioned several times, including for the vice arrests you asked me about, but nothing stuck. He died in '72. The son is clean apart from three speeding tickets.'

'Is there any indication how long his New York Street place had been operating as a brothel?'

'He said he had rented it out and that it was just a boarding house when he bought it in 1945.'

'Do you have an occupation for the son?'

'Self-employed. But it doesn't say at what.'

'Jerry, you are a friend. I'm grateful. I'll do something for you one of these days.'

'How about making it sooner rather than later,' he said. 'Considering you made me miss my train.'

His mournful tone gave me an idea.

I called Wendy Winslow of the Champaign Cable Company.

'Mr Samson!' she said. 'How pleased I am to hear from you! Are you interested in my proposition? I think it might be a real goer!'

Champaign may or may not be bubbly, but Ms Winslow certainly was.

'Can I ask you a question first?'

'But of course!'

'Is this a gag?'

She was silent for a moment. 'I don't know what kind of friends you have, Mr Samson, but my job is to open this franchise up. It's a tough market, so I have to offer my potential customers something different and better. Ideas are my strong point. One in ten comes to something. So I try to have a lot of them. I think there might be a nugget in what I suggested when I called you. If you are interested, I want to know.'

'Well, I'm not interested,' I said.

'Oh. All right. Have a good life, Mr Samson.'

'But, I know someone who might be.'

Miller left the copies of the arrest records in a sealed envelope at the Central Information desk the police maintain in the ground floor hallway of their wing of the City-County Building. The whole floor is a low security one, with easy public access to the Traffic Fines section, the Chaplain's Office and Missing Persons. There are elevators to the higher floors where they deal with the lower crimes, and a passageway to the City-County Tower and points administrative. The press room, with its ten tiny individual offices, is on the ground floor too.

The civilian on Information was suffering from something uncomfortable. He demanded identification before he would let me have Miller's envelope. I showed him my library card.

I took the files out for a sandwich and a cup of coffee at my mother's diner. It was a social visit, so I read the files through only once.

She closed up at eight and I helped to wash the day's last dishes.

I made light conversation not touching on the state of my employment. She talked mostly about her faraway grand-daughter and I left at eight-forty a sadder man.

Rovers Lounge was quiet and restful at nine except for the clap of a go-go dancer's tassle-tipped bosoms as they applauded themselves in time with muted music.

It was not a large place but there were tables as well as booths, a dance floor, a genuine coat check at the entrance and a couple of beefy gentlemen propping up walls like pugilistic statuary. Apart from the terpsichorean, I felt I'd walked into the past.

I made four men around a table and one couple in a booth to be the only paying trade. It seemed thin even for a Wednesday. But maybe it was the sort of place one went to after someplace else.

The sole barman sat on a stool reading a comic, but by the time my elbow hit a beer mat on the bar he was standing at attention in front of me.

I asked for Charlie.

'He's in the back. You know your way? First door past the john, on the left.'

I knocked, heard a muffled sound that I took for encouragement, and went in.

I faced a huge heavy man whose pouchy face and features were so menacing that I checked to make sure I had an unobstructed way back to the open door. He glanced up from thumbing through a stack of invoices and said, 'Hang on.'

I stood uneasily and watched him work. He sat at a wooden desk which was in the centre of a room whose walls were totally covered with framed autographed photographs of people shaking hands, turning to smile or lifting their cups to toast the lens.

Finally the man finished his work.

'Charlie Carson. I don't know you, do I?'

'No. There might have been a message that I was coming though. I called your home number and talked to a woman who said you'd be here tonight.'

'Ah,' he said appraisingly. His eyes and manners were as gentle as his visage was fierce. 'The singer.' He cocked his head in the manner of an experienced impresario. 'You must know how rough times are for singers who aren't sexy.'

'You haven't heard my voice,' I said.

He looked at me patiently.

I put him out of his misery. 'I'm not a singer.'

'Oh,' he said. 'Gladys told me but I forgot. I knew you was or you wasn't.'

I showed him my I.D.

He smiled a funny smile which I took for a 'you-look-the-part-but-I-didn't-believe-they-made-them-like-that-in-real-life' reaction.

'I'm trying to locate a woman. I have almost no lead on her and chances are that you won't be able to help either. The one lead I do have concerns a property you own.'

'Oh yeah? Which one is that?'

'A house on New York Street.'

He nodded and puffed out his cheeks for a moment. 'My slum,' he said.

'The woman lived there, years and years ago. In 1936 for sure but I don't know for how long before or after. I know you've only owned the place for ten or twelve years, but

73

your father had it before you, didn't he?'

The lips drew slightly tighter. 'That's right.'

'Is there any chance you could put me on to someone who might know about a woman who lived there in the thirties?'

'Pop didn't own the place till after the war,' Carson said cautiously. 'Do you know anything about the property?'

'I knew there were vice arrests there during your father's proprietorship.'

Carson just nodded. It would have been an opportunity to say that his father had had nothing to do with that sort of thing.

'You might, for instance, be able to tell me whether your father bought the house as a going concern,' I said.

'Naw. It was just a rooming house then. Not that I was involved in it. Neither when he bought it, because I was a kid, or later, because I don't play that way. But the old guy kept records and when he pegged out, I went through them all. Right from his own club days. He ran this place from 1931, you know, this very place. Kind of got swallowed up in the war. People spent more time working, in the defence plants and that, instead of partying their troubles away in clubs.' He gestured to the pictures around the wall. 'Most of these were his. Some surprising people have come out here, you know. Surprising who ends up in Indianapolis sometimes.'

I nodded, wondering whether to try to pull him back to my question, Wondering whether there was any answer worth pulling back to.

But Carson did it himself.

'Only other thing I know about that house was what he paid for it. He got it cheap.'

'What about records of any sitting tenants? I'm looking for anyone who might have been around when the woman I'm looking for was there.'

74

'I can check the rent books.'

'You have them?'

'Oh, yeah. A man's whole life is in things like that, ain't it? I can't throw that kind of stuff away.'

'I would be grateful. It is even possible that the woman I'm looking for was still there in 1945 herself. So if you could keep an eye out for the name, Daisy Wines, I'd appreciate it.'

He looked at me with a questioning frown. 'What was that name?'

'Daisy Wines. Do you know it?'

'I never heard the actual name,' he said.

Then he didn't say anything.

'But you reacted when I said it. What's that about?'

Carson leaned back. 'Well, when Pop ran this club here, he used to hire singers, you know?'

I glanced in the direction of his bar, thinking of the dancer who could hardly have been more mis-named as topless.

He knew what I was thinking. 'Yeah. Well, I hear sometimes today ain't that much different from those days, you know?'

'You were going to say something.'

'One of the things he did was give a lot of young kids breaks. This was while it was all still going pretty good for him. And maybe it was just by way of getting cheap acts, but he used to take these kids and let them sing or whatever and he used to give them stage names.'

I was listening attentively.

'And thing is, he always used to name them in connection with booze. Maybe to make people think drink? I don't know but it was part of the gimmick. I don't remember a Daisy Wines, but Ginny Tonic I remember, and Brandy Bottle, 'cause they both did pretty good for themselves. Brandy was still on the circuit until about five

75

years ago. Never sang again here, but I was going to bring her back, only she died. There was a lot of them went through that didn't make it. Pink Lady was another one.'

'Could you go through your records to see if there was a Daisy Wines?'

'Sure, sure. Glad to. Only the stuff is at home, not here. So it ain't going to be till, maybe, late afternoon tomorrow.'

'I would be very grateful,' I said with sincerity. Fearsome appearance notwithstanding, people didn't come more cooperative.

I ordered a drink before I left the Rovers. Out of my gratitude. But before I finished it I was aware that while when I'd come in I'd had a name for Paula Belter's mother, I was leaving not even sure I had that.

A term of six months' employment seemed very far away.

NINE

While I was out Douglas Belter had left a message to call him in the morning before eight-thirty, so I obliged by setting my alarm clock.

Being employed is corrupting. I tried to impress him by calling at ten past eight.

'I was rather expecting to hear from you last night,' he said.

'We didn't talk about how you wanted my reports. What suits you?'

'More often rather than less. Paula is pretty agitated about all this, and waiting uncertainly is a living death.'

Before I could respond he said, 'But I don't want you to call me at the office and would want to be here if you talked to Paula.'

'Sounds like mornings, evenings and weekends in some combination.'

'Yes.'

'I've pursued a number of lines,' I said, 'but I don't have substantive news yet. It is possible there may be one or two things of interest by the end of today.'

'I see.'

'Do you want me to call you tonight, then?'

He thought. 'Maybe you could come around,' he said. 'I feel it might be better to have you talk to Paula face to face.'

'I'll come tonight. About eight, unless I call to change the time.'

'Fine.'

There just hadn't been a place in the conversation for me to ask how he would react to my giving the case over to someone else.

I ate breakfast, read the newspaper and then drove through the light morning rain to North Meridian Street.

The building which had formerly housed two of the owners of the New York Street house could not have been a greater contrast to it. A vast two floor brick structure evenly balanced, side to side, behind the challenging tower which held the front door, it was immaculately maintained. And it was fronted by a design piece of flower beds and leafless shrubs ornately trimmed into geometric shapes. The centre of the area, an oval fishpond empty except for a small puddle of rainwater, stared at me like a Buddhaic eye. Plinths awaiting summer busts or decorative pots stood at the bottom of a ripple of stairs which led from the pond towards a flagpole, bare of salute, near the road. The whole place seemed to be in storage, waiting for warmer times.

As I turned back from front yard to house, my van seemed desperately out of key, a clanger in an otherwise perfectly executed scale.

I took a breath of humid air, resolved to forget myself, and pulled the handle marked 'bell'.

Inside I heard a bell, confirmation of the fundamental rationality of the world.

After a time locks were cleared. It took several seconds, however, before the front door opened and revealed a woman of about twenty-five in a fire-red dress cut about six inches above the knee. With a slightly pinched face ringed by braids of yellow hair and an otherwise Rubensesque body, she made a remarkable sight for a humble private eye to eye so early in a working day.

'Hello,' she said. She smiled.

'Are you the owner of this house?'

'Me? Miss Edwards?' She shook her head. 'No way,' she said.

'Miss Edwards is the owner?'

'That's right.'

'Is she related to the late George Bennett Raymond Edwards?'

'Couldn't tell you.'

'Is it possible for me to speak to Miss Edwards?'

She sucked on her lower lip, blinking her eyes in thought. 'I s'pose,' she said. 'What about?'

'I hope she will be able to help me with a little information.'

The girl seemed surprised. 'Miss Edwards?'

'That's right.'

'Do you know her?'

'No. Why?'

'Not much of a talker, Miss Edwards.'

'Would you mind asking her? I won't take much of her time and it's just possible that she could help me a lot.'

'Sure. O.K.,' the girl said. She pivoted sharply and slipped into the interior of the house.

I quickly tired of ducking drizzle drops on the front step. I crossed the threshold and, as a gesture of goodwill and energy conservation, closed the front door behind me as I passed from the entrance chamber of the tower into the front hall itself.

I needn't have worried about escaping heat. The place was virtually as cold inside as out, and the chilly atmosphere wasn't softened in the slightest by minimal furnishings and a bare stone floor.

I didn't get the opportunity to peer into the rooms which led off the hall, because the girl in the red dress returned from the back of the house quickly.

'Found your way in,' she said.

'I didn't know whether tradespeople were supposed to stay in the porch, but I decided to take a chance.'

'Oh, don't be like that,' she said with a flicker of sympathy. 'I'm just hired help here myself.'

'What do you do?' I asked.

'Personal secretary,' she said.

'And companion? That kind of thing?'

'No, no. I have a list of duties and there are special jobs sometimes. But we don't socialise. It's not for an employee to say, but she's pretty withdrawn. I get my room and board, and a lot of time to myself. Perfect for a writer.'

'You're a writer?'

'In the flesh,' she said.

'What sort of things do you write?'

'Non-fiction bestsellers,' she said.

I scratched my head. 'Would I know your name?'

'Oh, not yet. I'm still doing research for my first book. But you'll know it one day. Jane Smith.'

'Ah,' I said, nodding.

'Which,' she said more slowly, 'brings me to what I wanted to ask *you*. Do you know anything about maxi orgasms in men?'

'Excuse me?'

'There's been books like that done for women, see. But I'm working on it from the men's side of things. I've tracked down a technique for male multiple orgasm, when the guy holds back on the semen delivery after he's had the feeling. It's not necessary for them to be part of the same event, see.'

'Oh.'

'But now I'm on the trail of the male maxi. Doesn't ring a bell?'

'Sorry,' I said. 'Tone deaf.'

*

Miss Edwards received me in a glass enclosed porch which was, blessedly, warm. She was working at a large table which was covered with dried 'everlasting' flowers of several kinds. A few were soaking up to their heads in a shallow pan of water and the focus of the work was a green styrene block which was riddled with wires projecting in a fan of angles. A few of the flowers were already in place. Miss Edwards worked carefully, but dexterously, and was twining three stems.

She was a small woman, and lightly built. I put her somewhere in her late sixties or early seventies.

She didn't rush and I didn't make impatient sounds, but after a while she placed the flowers she had worked together on a rack and fixed their now joint stem in place with pins. She turned in her chair by means of three short movements to face me.

'Jane says you have something to say to me.' She spoke clearly and watched me with a concentration which in no way suggested inability to communicate. Perhaps if she didn't socialise with Jane Smith it was only because she had nothing to say to her.

'Yes,' I said. 'I'm grateful that you will allow me to interrupt you so early in the morning.'

A gold watch dangled as a pendant from a chain around her neck and she looked at it.

'This isn't early for me,' she said. 'I've been up for nearly five hours. How long have you been up?'

'About half that.'

'Should I thank you for getting out so early in your day to visit me?' She answered her own question. 'Of course not. Just who are you and what do you want?'

I explained that I was a private detective and that a client wanted me to find out what had happened to a woman.

'Private detective,' she repeated. 'This isn't one of those

81

ugly divorce situations, is it?'

'No, it's not.'

'Terrible, those things. Some investigators don't accept that sort of work. Do you?'

'I do if it's offered.'

'Ugly business,' she said, clearly tarring me with the subject. 'Ugly.' Then, again she said, 'Ugly.'

It stopped me for a moment.

But I said, 'The woman I'm looking for may be a relative of my client's and he wants to find her or find out about her. In 1936 she lived in a house which was bought by a man named George Bennett Raymond Edwards.'

I had been intending to continue, but Miss Edwards reacted so sharply that I stopped involuntarily.

She rose, eyes wide open, shocked. Her mouth worked, but without sound. She dropped back on to her chair. She raised her hands to her eyes and leaned forward.

'Benny,' she moaned. 'My poor Benny.' She sobbed.

It lasted a long time. But when she lowered her hands and sat back in her chair again, her eyelids remained closed.

She breathed deeply, and irregularly, but even before she seemed completely calm she said to me, 'What is your name again?'

I told her.

'Bennett was my only brother.'

'If—'

'You said that someone lived in a house. Who?'

'The name I have is Daisy Wines,' I said.

I saw, or thought I saw, a slight tremor. But wasn't certain whether it was reaction to the name or residue from the distress that mention of her brother had caused before.

I continued. 'But it is possible that Daisy Wines' – and I watched carefully as I said it again, but saw nothing – 'was a stage name and that she was a night-club performer. I

82

'haven't confirmed this yet though.'

'Yes . . . ?' she said, asking me to go on.

'The name doesn't mean anything to you?'

'To me? Certainly not. But, of course, I had virtually nothing to do with my brother's private life once he got married.' She opened her eyes. 'His wife murdered him, you know.'

'I didn't know,' I said.

'Shot him, in cold blood.'

I said nothing.

'In this room.'

Despite myself, I felt a wave of shock.

'Did . . . ? Was she . . . ?' I had begun to speak before I decided what to say.

'Scot free. Batted her eyelashes at the jury and walked out with a halo.'

I waited again.

'No comment about that?' she challenged.

'It's difficult to know what to say, Miss Edwards.'

'All men,' she said.

'Excuse me?'

'Twelve good men and true crawling over each other to let her go because of her pretty face and her innocent eyes. But of course, you wouldn't understand that, being a man yourself.'

'I would hope that if I were on a jury –'

'There was no *justice* at that trial.' She shook her head several times, short violent shakes. 'None at all. The only, tiny, saving grace was that she didn't get as much as she thought she would,' Miss Edwards said.

'As much what?'

'Money, of course. She got a fortune out of killing Benny, but not everything. Not this place. And maybe only half what she married him for. We kept her from that. We did.'

The memory of this limited success seemed to satisfy her

83

for the moment.

I used the pause to ask again, 'Would you know of anybody who might remember something about the people who lived in a house your brother owned? A lawyer or . . . anybody?'

'I know the house you mean,' she said.

'You do?'

'Benny only ever owned the one. A dreary little rooming establishment.' She paused. 'He bought it for her because she had a friend there, some sort of *concierge* I believe.'

'I've talked to Mrs Murchison.'

'Ah yes. Murchison.'

The name cued a reverie, and not a pleasant one. But after a moment Miss Edwards smiled slightly and said, 'You've talked to the Murchison woman. So she is still alive?'

'She's a resident at a nursing home called Biarritz House,' I said.

'And did she help you?'

'She is sometimes not very lucid. But I hope she will.'

'Still being looked after, no doubt,' Miss Edwards said sourly.

'Can you tell me about Mrs Murchison?' I asked.

'What? I hardly knew of her. My brother's employee.'

'You wouldn't,' I asked, 'happen to know the where-abouts of your brother's wife?'

'I always said that if I ever found her again I would kill her.' Miss Edwards shivered and shrugged. 'I haven't been put to the test. She left town after the miscarriage of justice. I never found her. Benny's lawyers know where she is but they won't tell me.'

'Who are they?'

'They won't tell you either.'

'But they might pass a message to her for me.'

She wagged her head as if I was being pedantic. 'They

were my lawyers too, but I dropped them when they wouldn't help me.' She pursed her lips, then said, 'Barker, McKay and Gay. They used to practise in the Wright Building, downtown. But of course, I don't know whether they're still in business.'

I said, 'I appreciate your talking to me very much, Miss Edwards.'

She was quiet for a moment before she said, 'I haven't talked about Benny for decades.'

'I'm sorry if I've upset you.'

'It is all so clear to me, so clear.' She hesitated. 'I should thank you for reminding me.' Then, 'That's it, is it? Well, I haven't helped you at all.'

'I'm grateful for your time.'

'Then if you come across my brother's wife, perhaps you will let me know where she is?'

'And make myself an accessory?'

She didn't smile. 'What danger could I be to her any more?' She sighed. 'Of course, she's probably married and killed off half a dozen other poor boys by now, so who can tell where she would be these days.'

Jane Smith, bestseller-to-be, popped out in front of me as I walked through the house towards the front door.

'You must have gotten on famously with her to stay that long. I can't remember a visitor since I began here who got near that much of her highness's time.'

I said, 'How long have you been here?'

'Six months next week. Hey, slow down. Can I ask you another question?'

Inside the tower, I stopped.

She needed no further invitation. 'What do you know about power parties?'

'About what?'

'Power parties. The host hires some people to come in

and act like kidnappers or psychos and wave guns around and make the guests do sexual things with each other. You ever been to one?'

TEN

On my way home I stopped at Barker, McKay and Gay, Attorneys at Law.

Whatever setback the loss of Miss Edwards as a client had represented, the exterior trappings of the partnership hadn't suffered. The pile of the carpet came over the sides of my shoes and tickled me through my socks.

I explained to the receptionist that I wanted a brief word with whoever dealt with the affairs of Mrs George Bennett Raymond Edwards.

The receptionist sent a note to a secretary who sent it to a clerk who sent it back to a secretary. The ascertaining of who was responsible for what took five minutes, an age compared to the time it took for a tall slim grey-haired man to come looking for me once the memo had been passed to an inner office.

He introduced himself as P. Donald Barker and asked, 'What would your business with Mrs Edwards be, Mr Samson?'

'I would like to speak to her,' I said.

'That is not possible.'

'Why not?'

'It is, simply, not possible.'

His tone of voice suggested I could have been a President for all the chance I had to get a change in reaction. Democratic exclusion, if nothing else.

I described what I was trying to do and the slimness of

the chance that Mrs Edwards could help. The fact that my interest was not in Mrs Edwards herself relaxed Barker slightly and when I suggested that he might pass on a message if I wrote one, he said he would pass it to the 'appropriate member of the firm for consideration'.

I didn't know what to make of that but it was the best offer I was going to get.

Barker obtained some paper for me and I spent several minutes writing a request for information about the residents of the New York Street house. I wrote in my best handwriting and offered to visit Mrs Edwards anytime, anywhere, if she would be willing to see me.

'Anytime, anywhere,' rang artificially enthusiastic, but, after all, I was to 'spare no expense.'

And, I was curious to know if she *had* killed off six more husbands since 1940.

There was a message on the machine to call Miller when I got back.

'I'm getting worried about you,' I said. 'Don't you ever go out on cases?'

'Sometimes,' he said, but there was an element of reserve in his voice which made me wonder if I had stumbled on to an issue.

He didn't give me a chance to push it, even if I had been inclined to. He said, 'What's this Champaign Cable Company business?'

'They called you?'

'Yeah, they called me.'

'Then you probably know more about it than I do.'

He hesitated. 'So, it's not a joke? Tell me straight, Al. If you're screwing around, tell me.'

'They called me, and I passed them on to you because you are discontented with what you're doing. Any screwing around is strictly their responsibility.'

He seemed to think about what I said. Then, 'I'm going out to lunch with this Winslow woman today. It can't hurt.'

'No,' I agreed.

Wishing not to be pressed further on the ambitions and hopes which had sprung fresh born from Wendy Winslow's phone call, Miller said, 'How's your work going?'

'Slowly. I might have some more names to be checked through soon, if you don't mind.'

'Whatever you like,' he said, but I had the feeling that his mind was elsewhere. In a limelight, perhaps.

I called Maude at the *Star*.

'Mr Samson,' she said, in a tone of voice which acknowledged that it was rare for me to contact her twice in a month, much less twice in a week. 'Things must be looking up.'

She has known me when my economic situation was even worse. But we both like to forget those days.

'I want you to examine what you have on a Daisy Wines. She might have been a night-club performer in the thirties.'

'I see.'

She waited. 'Is that it?'

I hadn't planned it, but on impulse I said, 'There was a murder case in 1940 that I want to know about. A Mrs George Bennett Raymond Edwards was tried and acquitted of killing a Mr of the same name. It would have been front-page stuff because they had money.'

'Oh, yes?'

'And while you are at it, have a look for a Miss Edwards, sister of the deceased, and a man called Normal Bates.'

'I'm pleased for you,' she said after saying she would get to work on it later in the afternoon.

I sat at my desk and wondered whether I should worry about the ease with which I was becoming able to spend other people's money. Even to satisfy my curiosity, once I got in the mood.

In the early afternoon I managed to find out that the other former owner of the New York Street house, S. H. Garrison, had died in 1948. I tracked down a granddaughter who convinced me that I would have little hope of getting any kind of lead through Garrison relatives.

Then I spent some time musing on the state of play. I had requests for information about Daisy Wines out with Charlie Carson and with Maude. If they both came up as blank as Miller had, I could, perhaps, go to the Belters and regretfully sign off the case. Next stop Normal Bates, regular employment, riches.

I decided I would call Bates to tell him that it was possible I would be free by the end of the day.

But I didn't get a chance because I heard someone come into my outer office. I straightened the papers on my desk, and put away the pad I was doodling on.

Whoever it was began to play my piano.

I don't know music. Occasionally I pick at the thing, when I'm looking for a way to break the silence of the phone not ringing.

But this was the genuine article. Classical stuff. More than one note at a time.

I stayed in my inner office while the melancholia of the first piece ran into frenetic jig-joy in a second.

Quietly, I opened the door and went out to sit and watch and listen as the woman in the music seat played a sequence of short pieces which continued to alternate from what I would call happy to what I would call sad. After twenty minutes I began to feel the difference between the two blurring.

Quite suddenly, the playing stopped and the woman turned the straight chair to face me.

In an assured but distracted way, Paula Belter said, 'I came by earlier. You were out.'

'Yes,' I said.

She said, 'I am restless at home. Tamae has cancelled all my lessons. Earlier, after I went away, I found myself thinking about your piano. It is a lot like one I had for a while when I was learning. It needs tuning, you know.'

'I'm not surprised.'

She turned to the keyboard and played some scales. She turned back to me as if there had been no interruption and said, 'I've been thinking about my childhood. I think my "mother" always felt a distance from me. And I know that her husband did, before he died.'

Not knowing what she wanted, I said, 'You were lonely then?'

She accepted the question as a perception, as if we had talked of such things before. She said, 'I've only begun to realise just how little of my childhood I remember before I started playing the piano. I never think about it. I never talk about it. I remember that big boarding house, now I've been to see it.' For a moment she gazed at me, or rather through me, as if seeing something a mile away. 'But it was, it is, almost unfamiliar. From the outside anyway. I remember having some corners, secret places where I would read and hide. And I remember the kitchen. We had a wooden table and I used to get splinters from it sometimes. And I liked cherry pie. I *loved* cherry pie. And I used to play in a big empty lot a couple of blocks away, but it isn't there any more. And there was a little girl called Lorraine McKenzie who used to have a dirty face all the time and take my hand and we'd go hunt for boys and throw stones at them. I remember all these things, but I don't feel that I *know* them, not really. I don't feel intimately familiar with my life there. I don't quite feel that I was one of the people living there.'

Suddenly she closed her eyes and tilted her head back and opened her mouth and spouted a deep breath in the manner of a whale sounding.

'Dear oh dear. What I came to tell you about was Aunt Vee.'

'Aunt Vee?'

She looked at me again. 'There was a woman who visited my "mother". Whenever she came I would be called from wherever I was. I didn't mind, because she gave me candy. I wonder now whether she was my mother. My biological mother, I mean, rather than the one who raised me.' She ran a little finger around the inside of one of her cheeks for several seconds. 'I don't know how "Vee" fits from Daisy, but when I was looking at the house I remembered her. For what it's worth.'

'Do you remember anything else about her?'

'A green scarf with a pattern on it. I suppose it was a paisley pattern with bits of red and yellow. And she wore some rings, but I don't know whether they were real or not.'

'Colour of hair? Tall or short?'

She shrugged.

'Age?'

'Oh, younger than my mother. My – well, you know what I mean.'

'How often did she come?'

'Not very often. And she didn't come after I was about five or six.'

'Not at all?'

'I don't remember her after I started school. There were some dresses I wore at kindergarten. She brought them but I'm sure that she never came again.'

'At least,' I said, 'it is a new name to try on Mrs Murchison.'

Mention of Mrs Murchison made Paula Belter visibly uneasy and sad. She nodded slowly.

'Mrs Belter, do you remember anybody else from those

days?'

'What do you mean?'

'It might help if I could locate someone who lived in the boarding house around the time that Daisy Wines did who knew her or knew of her.'

'I see.' She locked her hands behind her neck and pressed her elbows together in front of her chin. 'I don't know,' she said. 'There was a man who I thought was a cowboy, because he had that kind of boots, you know. I don't remember his name.' She squinted. 'I don't know. My brain hurts. I'll think about it for you. I don't recall there being many people living there as I got older. There certainly weren't many when we moved. Doug says that you are coming to the house tonight.'

'That's right.'

'I'll try to think by then.'

She closed her eyes and breathed deeply in the chair.

Opening them for a moment, she asked, 'Is there somewhere I can lie down?'

Having little option, I led her to my bedroom. I tried to pull the covers from the floor over the sheets, but she moved quickly and seemed to fall sidelong into the hollow which was exposed.

She closed her eyes and said, 'Thank you.'

'That's quite all right.'

She reached towards me, I thought for the blankets I was holding, and I stopped to put them over her. But she found my hand and pulled at it. At first I sat beside her but it was clear that she wanted me to lie beside her and I did so for a while, until she relaxed into sleep.

I watched her breathe for a time. Then I rose carefully and went back to my inner office and sat at my desk.

Half an hour later I heard the outer door open and close.

ELEVEN

Charlie Carson seemed pleased to see me when I arrived a little after five. 'I think you gonna be happy,' he said.

He led me through his house to a small brick extension at the back behind the garage. The walls were as filled with folders and papers on shelves as those in his club office had been with photographs.

Carson smiled almost embarrassedly. 'I kinda keep things. Gladys says I ain't never thrown nothing away, which ain't far off the truth. But if I can afford it and I enjoy it, well, where's the harm?'

We stepped carefully over boxes on the floor to find two chairs at a small desk. Carson pulled out two scrapbooks, and a wages ledger.

'Daisy Wines, you said.'

'That's right.'

He talked as he leafed through one of the scrapbooks. 'She was a singer. Never real good, because she didn't draw much money, but on the other hand good enough she worked for my old man more than three years. Probably didn't work nowhere else, maybe rested two weeks out of four part of the year and worked through other parts. I could figure it all out for you, because I have his wages books.'

He found the scrapbook page he was looking for. 'There she is.' He turned the volume for me to see better and pointed to a newspaper clipping from the *Star* that comprised an advertisement for The Hideout, a club then on West Washington Street. There were three pictures of entertainers 'performing nightly', one of whom was 'that pretty little Miss, Daisy Wines'.

The picture was small, and not terribly clear, but showed a young blonde woman smiling shyly.

'This book is for 1936. The only other thing I got by way of Daisy Wines is a picture from 1938.' He opened the other scrapbook and leafed lovingly about a third of the way through. This time he stopped at a black and white photograph of revellers at a club table.

Carson said, 'I told you before about Ginny, right?'

'Ginny Tonic,' I said. 'Yes.'

'Well, this is a picture of Ginny having a drink with my old man.' He pointed to a man whose stubby, round, rough body sat merely as a pedestal for a compelling face with silent-movie eyes and black, straight hair. The woman with him was full-featured with a wide happy mouth.

'They was friends, him and Ginny, but she left the circuit –must have been soon after this picture – and never worked around here again.'

'And?' I said.

'Well, see this girl down the table . . . ?'

And I could tell, now that he pointed her out, that it was Daisy Wines. Older than in the first photograph, but, if anything, looking even less worldly with a genuine fair complexion and blonde hair.

There was another woman at the table and two other men. I asked whether he knew who they were.

'No,' he said. 'All civilians.' He thought for a moment. 'I might be able to work it out if I go through the books looking for them, maybe in other shots. It's possible.'

'Would you mind?'

'I'd like it. Jees, I flick through them a lot anyhow, but it will keep Gladys off my back to be doing it for somebody.'

'And I would like to borrow the photograph, if I may.'

'I thought you might want it,' Carson said thoughtfully. 'I don't like to lend these things out or mess up the books.'

'I can understand that.'

'You'll have to sign a receipt and leave me fifty bucks as an incentive, kinda, to bring it back. Sorry, but I won't be happy otherwise.'

'All right,' I said. 'I just hope I've got the cash on me.'

We settled on thirty-nine fifty. I handled the photograph carefully, putting it inside the hard cover of my notebook as I prepared to go.

Carson looked at me.

'What?' I said.

'That all? Don't you want something else?'

'Yeah,' I said. 'What?'

'How about Ginny's address?'

The address was for a tiny board-sided bungalow in a dead-end street off Bethel Avenue, the south-east side of town. It was porchless and painted in faded lavender and sat on a plot of ground which ran to about five feet on each of the four box sides.

I knocked at the door and it was opened immediately by a woman as big and round as the house was small and square. 'Hi, there,' she said.

'Miss Tonic?'

'Why, I sure am, honey. Even if nobody much knows it these days. Hey, why'n't you come on in.' She stepped back and I entered. There were two chairs in the chintzed and laced and frilled sitting room. 'Sit down, sit down.'

I sat down.

She poured me a drink. After giving it to me she topped up another, already seemingly a double, and sat down facing me. She drank deeply, plumped a cushion at the back of her head and said, 'Ah, that's more comfy. I got a call, out of the blue, from Charlie Carson about you. I nearly fell on my backside. He was only a run-around kid when I first met him, you know. God, it brings it back. Anyhow, Charlie said you might be coming around. I didn't want to start before you, but I tell you, honey, I don't usually wait for the sun to get this low before I have a little drink, you know?'

'Many thanks,' I said and sipped. It was undiluted vodka. 'Not living up to your name these days, then?'

'Naw. Don't mind gin, but the tonic makes me all bubbly inside. So I give it up for Lent. About twenty years ago.' She laughed loudly.

When she finished she shrugged and said, 'The flavour kind of gets me down. Vodka's straighter. You know where you are.' She sighed. 'Charlie said you're looking for Daisy Wines.'

'That's right.'

'Cute little kid.'

'Do you know where she is?'

'God, no. I haven't seen her for years. I didn't even know where she lived when I knew her, if you get me. I never did know her very well. Charlie didn't say I did, did he?'

'No.'

'That's all right. Naw, that was kind of my heyday, you know? Now is more my hay day because I sleep a lot. More and more, and alone, more's the pity.' She laughed again easily and tossed her hair from her eyes. Grey now, it had been dark in the photograph and I could see why, if she could sing too, she had enjoyed a popularity.

She said, 'I knew Daisy only from having her start to sing in The Hideout when I wanted to take some time off. She was a tiny little kid. Not short so much as skinny. No meat on her and if there was anybody who was ever a change from me it was her.'

'Do you know where she came from?'

'She lived somewhere in town. Everybody wanted to know if she was old enough to work in a place like The Hideout. She looked maybe thirteen. But I suppose she was sweet sixteen and . . .' She stopped.

'Yes?'

'Now that you mention it, I remember thinking that she sounded like she was fresh off the farm. The way she talked, you get me? I figured her for a real little country gal. Maybe she just up and moved to the big city. Yeah, that was probably it. But she had her a real sweet voice, and not quiet. It was no glass-rattler, but she could sing over the drunks and she got a bit of style as things went on.'

'Charlie has a picture of her from The Hideout from 1936. Was that when she began?'

'Yeah,' she said unhesitatingly.

I smiled.

'You wonder how come I'm so sure. Well, I had kind of personal reasons to take some time off in '36. I took a few weeks to St Louis with a guy I thought I had plans with. They didn't work out but I remember the year 'cause of that.'

'Sorry things didn't go well.'

She wrinkled her nose. 'Guy got machine-gunned to death, machine-gunned no less, a couple of years later.' She shivered and drank. 'So many holes that his blood didn't know which ones to leave by.' She leaned back. 'A year and a bit after I got back from St Lou I went to Texas. I worked down there mostly ever since. Houston in the war and Fort Worth after. I packed it in a few years ago and came back here.'

'The name you were born with wasn't Ginny Tonic?'

'Uh no,' she said. 'The Ginny is mine right enough, but they had to force the tonic on me.'

'So Daisy Wines was unlikely to be the girl's real name?'

'Right. Mike – that's Charlie's father – he gave us these

98

names. Did Charlie explain?'

'Yes. But you said you were Ginny already?'

'Virginia, yeah. Must have been after the state.'

'Does that mean there would be a good chance that Daisy was the girl's real name?'

She shook her head. 'Not really. More likely the kid came in for an audition with a daisy in her hair and Mike was drinking a glass of wine at the time.'

'I see.'

'I'm sorry. I never did know her that good, nor nothing much personal about her.' And she stopped.

'Something come back?'

'She had a boyfriend. Well, I mean there were always a lot of guys hanging around club singers then, you know.' She raised her eyebrows. 'And around the dancers. And waitresses. And hat check girls. Jees, just think. Every guy around used to wear a hat. How many hats do you see nowadays?'

I took Charlie Carson's photograph from my notebook and handed it to her.

She stared at it a long time.

I asked, 'Is that Daisy's boyfriend?'

Absently she said, 'What? Oh. Yeah. I was looking at me. God, that was a long time ago. I wasn't a bad-looking broad.'

'You're not a bad-looking broad now,' I said.

'Yeah, yeah,' she said dismissively. Then she looked up. 'You know I was singing until a few years back?'

'You said.'

'I've got like I was made out of pink pumpkins since I stopped. I didn't want to quit, but my voice began to crack and hurt and it's no good like that. So I packed up and came back where I started. I looked up Mike's boy. Hell of a guy, Mike. Didn't forget you. Helped you if he could. If you was a friend. Rough bastard if you wasn't. But I was.

99

Good kid too, Charlie.'

'Did you set much money aside?'

'Not much. Some. I *had* money, mind you. Oh yeah, a lot of good money passed through my pudgy little fingers. But there are expenses too, to keep things going. Especially later on.' She pushed up lightly on her cheeks with her finger tips. 'Like my face. This old thing has been lifted so often it ought to float away like a goddamn helium balloon.'

'You said the guy in the picture was Daisy's boyfriend.'

'Yep.'

'Which guy?'

She picked the more obscured of the two men who were not Michael Carson. There was little distinguishing about him. In his twenties, dark hair. Smiling less than the others.

'Do you know who he was?'

She shook her head. 'Sorry. I'd like to help more. All I know was that he seemed to have plenty of money, that he was crazy about her and wanted to marry her.'

'Wanted to marry her or to become better acquainted?' I asked.

'Marry is what I heard. Though those was definitely the days of the good girls and the bad girls and we was usually considered bad girls. I don't know. It's only information I remember hearing kind of sideways since I was more involved with my own . . . engagements, if you get me.'

'Did you ever hear of Daisy having a child?'

'A child? Daisy? No. I never heard that. Why?'

'I just wondered.'

'As far as I knew Daisy didn't know what it took to make a baby. Not that there weren't plenty of fellas around, from the boss on down, willing to help a girl out on that part of her education.'

'Country girls usually have at least a theoretical knowledge pretty early on,' I said.

'That's true,' she said. 'But if Daisy knew how she didn't

go in for practising.'

'What do you mean?'

'I said she had this guy hanging around her all the time.'

'Yes.'

'Guy with money.' She handed the picture back. 'Not a bad-looking guy. Young. Well, in those days, in the kind of situation we was in, guys like that didn't show up every day. Not for many of us. Well, all I know is that word was she wouldn't let him touch her, you know what I mean? And she wouldn't take nothing off him, no presents. There are some guys who maybe like that, and I couldn't tell you if in the long run he was one of them. But I can tell you for fact that in those days, around The Hideout, there wasn't many girls that had the nerve to play it like that for very long.'

'And Daisy did?'

'That's how I recall it.' She drained her glass. 'But God, I don't know if I'm remembering more than I remember, if you get me. Honest, I didn't know the kid very good.'

'I know you didn't know her real name, but does something beginning with "V" ring any bells?'

'"V"? Like in victory?'

I nodded.

She shrugged. 'Hey, I'm going to have another little drink. You keep me company?'

'I think I would enjoy that,' I said, 'but I've got to go see some people.'

'O.K. Yeah.'

'One last thing.'

'Shoot.'

'Do you know where I could find anyone else from those days who knew Daisy?'

'Oh yeah,' she said positively. 'Lots of them.'

'Where?'

'In the graveyard, honey. I open the papers and I read a

101

name and I remember it just in time to say goodbye. I'm a dying breed. Better ask your questions now.' And without again inviting me to stay, she rose to refill her glass.

TWELVE

I was due to call on the Belters and intended to arrive there sooner rather than later. Even so, I drove home first, to catch a bite to eat and smack my face a few times to freshen up. We're a rough, tough lot, private eyes. When I have more time I bang my head against a wall.

There had been considerable action on my telephone while I was out. I had messages to call back Miller, Maude, my lady friend, and my mother. While thinking about who to honour first, the telephone beat me to it and rang itself.

It was Douglas Belter.

'I am almost on my way,' I said.

'Don't.'

'What?'

'Please don't come here tonight.' His voice was always controlled but this time it sounded particularly steely.

I hesitated before speaking.

'If it's not convenient . . .' I began uneasily.

'Paula's mother, Ella Murchison, died this afternoon. We are in considerable turmoil.'

'She died? What of?'

'She went to sleep some time after lunch and just died.'

'Was she unwell?'

'Not particularly. Except that she was generally not very well. You met her.'

'Yes.'

'We are full of making arrangements tonight.'

103

'Yes. I can understand that.' Belatedly perhaps, I said, 'Please accept my condolences.'

'Thank you,' he said. 'I will call again when we have ourselves straightened out.'

I sat by the phone doing nothing for what felt a long time.

After a while I thought again about making the return calls which were due.

Instead I went out, to Biarritz House.

It was not apparently buzzing with activity. There were few cars in the visitors' parking spaces and hardly anyone in the foyer.

The nurse at the reception desk was new to me. I asked for Connie Howard.

'She's not on duty now. Can I take a message? Or is there someone else who can help you?'

'One of your residents died here today.'

The nurse switched a gear. I guess I hadn't looked at first like a grieving relative.

'In fact, two of our people unfortunately have passed over. We have had a real sorry time.'

'I'm speaking of Mrs Ella Murchison.'

The woman nodded sympathetically.

'Is the doctor who issued the death certificate on the premises?'

She was somewhat taken aback. 'Why . . .' she stopped as she decided what to say. 'I'm not sure.'

I took that to mean that he was around.

'I need to speak to him about the cause of death,' I said. 'Nothing complicated.'

'Mrs Murchison's family was in here this afternoon. I'm sure that they have all the necessary information. What was your relationship to Mrs Murchison, please?'

'I work for the family,' I said, 'and there are a few details

104

that I still would like to have. What with the turmoil, and everything. You know. I won't take much of the doctor's time.'

'I'll call around to see if Doctor Bentonworth is still on the premises.'

He was. I joined him in a windowed corner of the dining room. The evening meal for ambulatory residents was over and, except for a boy at the other end of the room who was refilling sugar bowls, we were alone.

Bentonworth was a gaunt man in his late thirties, who hunched over his coffee cup as if his shoulder blades hung from a wire running down from the ceiling.

I sat across from him and he took a slow slurp from his cup before saying, 'You wanted to see me?'

I introduced myself and said that I worked for the Belter family.

'Oh, yes?' he said. He looked at me. His eyes were bloodshot.

'What exactly did Ella Murchison die of?'

He looked again. Raised an eyebrow momentarily, dropped it back in place and said, 'Heart failure.'

'Did she have a history of heart trouble?'

'No.'

'Were you her regular physician?'

'She had her own doctor, as do most patients here. But if you mean did I know her medical history, I did. I do.'

'Was she unwell?'

'Not particularly.'

'Was her death expected?'

'No.'

'Will there be a post mortem?'

'No.'

'Shouldn't there be?'

'Why?'

'To find out why she died when she wasn't expected to.'

105

'There is nothing suspicious about her death. People of eighty-seven often just die one day.'

'How precisely did you determine the cause of death?'

'Her heart stopped.' He shrugged. 'Mr Samson, do you feel there are unusual circumstances associated with Mrs Murchison's passing? If so I would appreciate hearing why.'

'I believe that she was behaving strangely in the last few days.'

'In what way?'

'Some visitors, including myself, found that she became unresponsive when they tried to talk to her about certain events in the past. The nurse who knew her best said this vagueness was not typical of the lucidity problems she sometimes had.'

'To me you are conveying a change in behaviour which is consistent with sudden, if unexpected, death in old people. Slight changes in behaviour or voice are sometimes the only clues we have of alteration of condition. Frequently they are only recognisable in retrospect.'

'I can understand that,' I said. 'But she was being asked to remember things that might be painful to her, things she would not have forgotten.'

'In which case, the additional emotional stress might be the underlying extra cause you are seeking. Unless you are implying that somebody murdered her.' He studied me closely. '*Is* that what you are implying?'

'I don't know,' I said. 'To me it just feels wrong.'

He looked at me in silence.

'Where is the body now?' I asked.

'The family has made arrangements.'

'I guess I'd better talk to them.'

He shrugged.

'I'm sorry if I've been a nuisance,' I said.

'I am used to nuisances,' Doctor Bentonworth said. He

sipped at his coffee, and made a face. 'Cold,' he said. He was still frowning as I left the room.

In the foyer I asked the reception nurse for Connie Howard's home address.

'I can't give you that. I'm sorry.'

'Would you call her at home and ask whether she would let me come by now, or at least talk on the phone about Mrs Murchison? If she says "no" then fair enough.'

Mrs Howard said 'yes.'

The address was a small apartment building less than two miles from Biarritz and Connie Howard greeted me in the entrance hall as I came in.

'I saw you coming up the walk,' she said.

Her apartment was on the first floor, in the front, where she had a good view of the street. I followed her in, and found a slim woman already sitting in an armchair cradling a half-full martini glass.

'This is my friend, Christine,' Connie Howard said.

'Hello.' Christine lifted her glass to me.

'How do you do?'

'Would you like a drink?'

'I think not,' I said. 'Thanks.'

'What can I do for you?'

Off duty, she projected rather less of the motherly organiser than when I'd met her at Biarritz House. 'I am wondering how you feel about the death today of Ella Murchison.'

Quietly, Mrs Howard said, 'It made me sad.'

'She liked Ella,' Christine said.

Baldly I said, 'The timing of her death feels wrong to me. I want to know if there was anything unusual about it. You knew her better than anybody else, so I thought I'd come and ask.'

107

'She seemed all right this morning.'

'Nothing gave you a clue she was about to die?'

'Not really.'

'How was her mind?'

Nodding, she said, 'All right.'

'Was her family in today?'

'Her daughter and the Japanese housekeeper spent a few minutes a little after ten. Not long stays.'

'And when did she die?'

'They think she went to sleep mid-afternoon. She never woke up. I found her about half past five.'

'Did she usually take a nap?'

'Now and then; not every day.'

'Did she show any signs of stress or of being bothered by the rush of visitors recently?'

Connie Howard sat back. 'There have been a lot, but if anything I felt it stimulated her. Old people suffer dreadfully from inattention. What isn't used doesn't work, by which I mean their minds, and I think that's the source of a lot of mental lapses.'

'So, she was all right as far as you knew.'

'Yes.'

'And you were surprised that she died.'

'Yes.'

'Suspiciously surprised?'

After considering a moment Mrs Howard said, 'I suppose not. I was sorry. But it happens.'

I scratched my head. 'All right.'

Christine, in the pause, said, 'Weren't you on the box the other night? A Tanya Wilkerson interview?'

'Yeah.'

'You'll never be a TV star, will you?'

'Thanks.'

Connie Howard asked, 'Was there anything else you wanted to know?'

'I guess not. Perhaps I'm trying to see what isn't there.'
'An occupational hazard?' she asked.

I left restless. I didn't much feel like making the telephone calls which I owed. When I thought of them, they seemed together a wall too high.

I am uneasy with unexpected death. I sat in the van a long time. But at the end, it still felt wrong.

I started the van and set off to drive home.

The physical activity of shifting gears and stopping at red lights took me out of my contemplative frame of mind. I finally made a decision, to stop at the Indianapolis *Star* on the chance of finding Maude Simmons.

As I made my way through the desks on her floor I saw the light in her office. People not being in wasn't today's problem.

Before the war, most stores in Indianapolis had their stock on shelves from floor to ceiling. Maude's office was not the same shape but the density of files and boxes and card indices and books was strictly in the traditional mould. She might have abandoned the green visor and the pencil collection behind the ear, but the sea of VDUs stopped outside her office and her typewriter wasn't vulnerable to power cuts.

She was bent over her desk as I came in and she didn't look up. She just said, 'Yeah?'

'You left a message I should call,' I said.

Slowly she lifted first her gaze and then her body. She leaned back.

'I thought I'd save the dime.'

'You sure they didn't disconnect you before you noticed?'

'Now, now. It isn't like that.'

'I forgot. You're in funds.' She assessed me. 'I trust you

109

are in funds . . .'

'Yes.'

She reached for a large blue folder and took out a notepad and some envelopes.

'This is real work you had me do,' she said. 'These people were active a long time ago. Nothing easy like picking up the phone and asking a couple of guys whether the mayor is gay. This was down in the tombs stuff. Out of my office stuff.'

I wanted to assure her that money was no object, but found I couldn't say the words out loud.

'The Edwards murder trial,' she said. She took one of the envelopes, opened it and withdrew a stack of photocopies.

'It was a big case, you were right. We had stories on it, for weeks, running up to and through the trial. You want a summary?'

I took out my notebook and opened it.

'O.K.,' Maude said. 'Date is April 21, 1940. Mrs George Bennett Raymond Edwards telephones the police at eleven thirty p.m. to say that she has just shot her husband to death. Considering that G. B. R. Edwards is the son and heir to a well-known quantity of money – a kid like you may not have heard of the Edwards Meat Company, because it was bought out after the war, but it was bigger than Stark and Wetzell then, if you remember Stark and Wetzell. Anyway, the police arrive to find Mr Edwards dead with two holes in him, body on the conservatory floor, Mrs Edwards with bruises on her arms, a cut lip and a torn dress. She says he was beating her and she shot him in self-defence. They arrest her, hold her and, without much delay, try her for murder.'

'Nice,' I said.

'At the trial there was a lot of character and background testimony. They were married less than two years and weren't getting along. He accused her of fooling around.

She said he demanded unusual things of her which she did her best to comply with. Counsel asked for details, and got them, which was pretty shocking in those days. And it was clear that Edwards was a pretty strange character. A reputation as he grew up as a boozer, gambler and whorer in the kind of rich-kid fashion that doesn't date. An apartment on the near north side where he kept women, over a period of years. But it stopped when he married. She was younger. Like eighteen, with him whatever it works out . . .' Maude squinted at a page and found her date. 'Born January 19th, 1911, which made him twenty-seven when he married and twenty-nine when he died. You with me?'

I caught up with my notes and said, 'Yes.'

'As soon as they married he started making a public project out of his reformation, his devotion to his wife, his regrets for the excesses of younger years. Everything except something simple like fixing on a career and by the time they'd been married a year there were rumblings that his "spirit" wasn't quite in harness. There was quite a bit of defence testimony about tendencies to secrecy and unpalatable associations.'

'What about the prosecution?'

'Made something of the fact that she fired two shots instead of just one, and that both hit him in the region of the heart.'

'Whose gun?'

'Hers.'

'And her injuries?'

'Prosecution said self-inflicted. Defence said not. Experts from each side agreed the possibility of the other side's case. Inconclusive.'

'How close were the shots fired from?'

'Very close. But disagreement on what it proved.'

I said, 'I know she was found not guilty but what tipped it? I've been told it was an all-male jury and that she batted her eyelashes.'

'Probably something to that, but a key witness was from the Horse Thief Detective Association.'

'The what?'

'A detective agency.'

'The witness was a P.I.?'

'Hired by the deceased to establish how the accused spent her spare time. With particular attention to male companions.'

'And?'

'And she rated a completely clean bill of health. The guy followed her for nearly four months and didn't get an eyebrow out of place. He'd filed a string of blank reports, all of which were entered in evidence – along with Edwards' responses saying that he was still absolutely certain she was cheating. He didn't go quite as far as asking them to fabricate a little something.'

'And so they didn't. It's a noble profession, Maude,' I said.

She sat back and flipped through her notepad. 'While we're talking about him, that is virtually all the information I could find. I only looked for the easy stuff, since I was concentrating on the murder case. I can try to find out if there's anything else.'

I looked at her. 'You've lost me,' I said.

'Normal Bates. He *was* one of the people I was checking for you.'

'Bates?' I must have looked as blank as I felt.

'Normal Bates was the P.I. on the Edwards case.'

I said, 'I didn't know.'

'I thought this was *all* about the Edwards business.'

She looked at me as I sorted through the meaning of what she was saying.

I said, 'Daisy Wines?'

'Mrs Edwards.' She paused. 'You must have known *that*.'

THIRTEEN

I put my pen down and closed my hanging jaw by resting it on folded hands. It is a posture I adopt to look like I'm thinking.

'I didn't know,' I said.

'They were all names from the same pie,' Maude said. 'Why else . . . ?' She began, but didn't finish her sentence.

I picked up my pen again. 'Let's do this in short simple sentences, spoken slowly.'

'Born Vera Wert, in Logansport in—'

I interrupted. 'Vera?'

'That's right. Ready?'

'Yeah.'

'Born in 1920. For some reason I don't have the date. She came to Indianapolis in 1936 and became a moderately successful club singer with a little-girl-lost kind of style. O.K.?'

'Yeah.'

'Rich kid Edwards spotted her singing. Probably one day when he thought he was slumming. He courted her, for getting on to a couple of years. It is said that she was reluctant to marry him, because of the difference in their stations.'

'By whom?'

'Her own testimony.'

'She went in the box?'

'She did indeed. Our reporter thought she did pretty well.'

'Is your reporter still around?'

She smiled and shook her head. 'Sub-editing God's in-house news sheet.'

'Vera Wert,' I said.

'Married Edwards on June 28th, 1938. His family hated it.'

'What family was there?'

She looked at her notepad. 'A father who was not very well. Died in 1944. A sister.' She looked at me. 'You *had* to have known that Wanda Edwards was George Bennett Raymond's sister . . .'

'Yes,' I said.

'And that when Vera was acquitted she tried to shoot her . . .'

'The hell she did!'

'She put a slug into the courtroom ceiling. All dealt with quietly afterwards. She never came to trial.' Maude looked at her notes again. 'The sister never married, as far as I know. Looked after her father, who was . . . seventy-six when he died.'

'His wife?'

'Died when George Bennett Raymond was born. The old man never remarried. I don't know whether there is any additional information to be had about post-marital social life, but I don't have any.'

'I don't think it's important to me,' I said.

'O.K.,' Maude said. 'So George and Vera got married, without family blessing, but with family participation. They made a big splash, notable for the lack of celebration which pervaded the reception party.'

'Vera Wert's family?'

'Not on the guest list,' she said. 'I don't have anything about Vera before the murder except from our reports from the trial. Excuse me, I shouldn't say "murder". The

114

"shooting". And little after, because the young couple didn't have much social life. The upper crust was not generous to wives with Mrs Edwards' background.'

'We're talking late on in the depression,' I said. 'Was there much social life for them to be excluded from?'

Maude leaned back. 'Oh, yes. There was a whole season of dances. If anything it was more active than when times were economically better. Young men couldn't marry as early as they did before, and the dances were the main contact between expanded pools of unmarried young ladies and gentlemen. And the young marrieds were involved too.'

'All right,' I said. 'They got married. They got snubbed. They stopped getting along. He became strange, or maybe just stranger. He suspected her of playing around.'

'You said simple sentences . . .'

'So, on April 21st, she shoots him. What is known about that night?'

'Uncontested, that Edwards learned early in the evening that Mrs E. was pregnant. Family doctor stopped by. Vera was out, so he told Edwards. This led Edwards to be upset and he told his sister emphatically that it could not be his child.'

'That sounds a bit rough.'

'So did the sister's testimony about Mrs Edwards, but it was made completely clear that she had resented her sister-in-law from the beginning and probably the prejudice undercut what she had to say.'

'Mrs Edwards wasn't there when her husband learned about the pregnancy? Don't doctors tell the mother-to-be first?'

'I suspect some of the niceties become blurred when you're dealing with that kind of money.' Maude consulted a notepad. 'There was a houseboy who testified as to when Mrs Edwards got home. Just after ten.'

'Where had she been?'

'At a concert.'

'With someone?'

'Alone.'

I made a face.

Maude said, 'A maid testified too, agreeing about the time of Mrs Edwards' return, and saying that she seemed edgy, but not more than normal. Mrs Edwards testified that after she got home she and her husband had an argument about his jealousy. No one seems to have heard this. The bedrooms and the servants' room were all a considerable distance from the conservatory.'

I nodded.

'Mrs Edwards said that her husband began to beat her in his rage, and that she took her gun out to scare him. It didn't. They fought, it went off twice.'

'She carried a gun around?'

'She said that she often did.'

'Jesus,' I said. 'She just happened to have her gun handy. How did she pass that off?'

'Must be the way she told it,' Maude said.

'And is that it?'

'More or less. She called the police as soon as it happened. Nobody seems to have contested that there was no delay.'

'A big question for me now, Maude,' I said.

'Yeah?'

'What happened to her after the trial?'

'Apart from acting as a target for her aggrieved sister-in-law?'

I nodded.

'I don't have anything,' she said simply. 'Either as Mrs Edwards, or as Daisy Wines. The only suggestion is in one of the last stories. When she got off, she was asked what she was planning to do. She said that she was going to go away

116

for a while.'

'And that's it?'

'That's it.'

I said, 'I want to locate her.'

'Well, if she's not in Indianapolis, that only leaves the rest of the world.'

'I know who knows where she is. But they're not telling.'

'Oh?'

'Her lawyers.'

'Who are they?'

'Barker, McKay and Gay.'

Maude nodded slowly. 'I know old Ken Gay. I'll try but I don't think I can give you much hope.'

'I suddenly feel terribly tired,' I said.

'Let me give you the rest of what I've got. Then you can go collapse somewhere else.'

'O.K.'

'Wanda Edwards. Still lives in the family home. You know where that is?'

'I've been there,' I said.

Maude raised her eyebrows. 'I'm impressed, because she's been virtually a recluse since 1940. All my information is negative. No club memberships. No charities.'

'I have no club memberships or charities either,' I said. It didn't merit a response. 'Normal Bates?'

'Private eyes don't leave much of a mark,' Maude said.

FOURTEEN

Before I left Maude, I talked to her about further inquiries
I wanted her to make for me. She was impressed. The bill I
was running up was bigger than for all the work she'd done
for me in the past put together. She was so impressed that
she didn't even ask for the cash due so far.

We talked about where to concentrate her efforts next.
We agreed on getting a copy of the trial record and on going
through the newspaper files looking for leads to where Mrs
Edwards had gone when she left Indianapolis. Maybe
identifying someone who didn't snub her during her short
married life. Maude also agreed to try to locate Vera Wert's
family in Logansport and to have a go at prising open the
address files at Barker, McKay and Gay.

All but the last were things I would perfectly well do for
myself, but time would be saved.

And I suddenly had a mass of other things churning
around in my mind.

Miller's house not far north of Fall Creek was closer to the
centre of town than those of most married lieutenants of
police in Indianapolis.

It was about a quarter to nine when I pulled up outside.
A light was on illuminating a vinyl hand in the front
window. The hand is a symbol of a self-help programme in
which carefully screened households make themselves
available as safe houses for children who run into trouble

118

on their way to or from school. It's a pragmatic and constructive programme, the need for which is its own comment on life in our city.

I rang the bell. It was so long before there was any reaction that I thought the house was safe from me. But the porch light finally came on and it was Miller who peered at me through a window panel which bordered the jamb.

He opened the door and said, 'What are you doing here?' It was not very welcoming, but I suspected that the lack of grace was a carry-over from whatever was going on inside the house when I interrupted.

'I'd like a few minutes of your time,' I said.

He considered this, and said, 'Wait out there.'

He closed the door and turned out the porch light.

I went back to the street and stood by my van.

After five minutes, which seemed like an hour in a neighbourhood that wasn't safe for children in daylight, Miller came out. 'We're going to Chicken Delight. O.K.?'

'Sure.'

We got into my van.

When I pulled away from the kerb, I said, 'You'll have to navigate.'

'Oh,' he said distractedly. 'Yeah. Left up here.'

We rode quietly for a few minutes. Then he said, 'Hey, where are you going?'

'What do you mean?'

'You should have taken that last right.'

Silently I made a U-turn.

'Left at the lights. You'll see it after a couple of blocks.'

We continued in silence. I parked in the Chicken Delight lot. We went inside.

'Let's have a cup of coffee,' Miller said. 'Then get some stuff for Janie before we head back. I'll say there were long lines.'

'I arrived at a bad time?'

'They're all bad times,' he said. 'Nothing special.'

His attention seemed elsewhere. I asked, 'How was your lunch with Wendy Winslow?'

He looked away. He took a breath. He looked back at me. He said, 'I'm in love.'

We took our coffees to a table in a corner far from the doors.

'Tell me I'm crazy,' he said, 'but I haven't been able to get her out of my mind all afternoon, all evening.'

'You're crazy,' I said, but without conviction. Feelings are far enough between in this life that they shouldn't be dismissed out of hand. After consideration, maybe, but not out of hand. 'Are you crazy?'

'I think I must be. All of a sudden I'm thinking about leaving home. Quitting my job.'

I didn't quite know what to ask.

I didn't need to. 'She's so understanding,' he said. 'That's what gets to me. With Janie everything I say is a battle because she isn't listening to the words, she's hearing stuff behind the words that I don't even think I'm saying.'

'So, are you going to be a television star?'

'I'm going to test for it,' he said. 'But if that doesn't work out, Wendy's sure there'll be a place for me in the production department. Getting the stories together.'

I looked at him. 'The money?'

He shrugged.

We sipped coffee. He looked dazed. I thought about the number of years he had in on the police force and what pension he would draw on them if he quit now.

I watched him gazing through the window into the depths of space. Time heals wounds, wounds heels, and also takes the shine off silver and love. He was a full-growed man. It wasn't my job, or my pleasure, to rein in his resurgent passions.

I said, 'I hope you remember who introduced you.'

120

'What? Oh, yeah. I'm grateful.'

'Grateful enough to arrange an autopsy?'

'What?'

'An old woman died this afternoon. She wasn't sick, just old. But nobody besides me seems very bothered about why she died. Maybe it's because she was sitting on some information I wanted, but I'd like to be sure of the cause of death.'

Miller frowned.

I said, 'It's easy enough to ask for an autopsy if death is unexpected, isn't it?'

'Yeah.'

'So, will you do it?'

He shrugged again. 'O.K.'

I gave him Ella Murchison's name and the number of Biarritz House. I wrote 'unexpected death' on the slip of paper, so that he didn't forget it.

'Al, what are you suggesting here?'

'I'm suggesting a woman died and we don't know why.'

'Oh,' he said.

'I've also got a new name for you to put through your computers.'

'What's that?'

'Vera Wert.'

He shrugged and became lost to my 'real' world again. I didn't have enough belief that mine was more real than his to fight it. I added the new name to the slip of paper.

I stopped at my lady's house on my way home.

I had thought to talk. Of Normal Bates. Of Daisy Wines/Vera Wert/Mrs Edwards. Of Mrs Murchison.

But when we got settled with a quiet drink I was happy to rest from the day's events and speculations and listen to her day and keep a little company.

*

I went home, before midnight.

As soon as I got in I made a hot, milky drink and trundled off to bed. I sipped it in the dark and was tired and slept.

I heard the rumblings and tinklings first in my dreams. They brought me to a mazy half-consciousness and I thought maybe I was dreaming a piano.

But it was too tuneless, too explosive, too shattering.

I realised the tinkling part was the breaking of glass.

Then it stopped for a moment and I was gulled into self-doubt. Maybe it had all been a dream.

But the voices were real. And the booming and the smashing began again.

I jumped out of bed and ran naked to the back door.

The noise, when I took a step into the yard, was deafening. The aural equivalent of passing from darkness into bright light: my ears were blinded.

I stood for nightmare moments, unmoving.

Then I stepped back inside the doorway and turned on the floodlights.

Two men, dressed black from head to toe, straightened like disturbed rabbits. Each carried a rifle. Each stood by a bay of broken glass.

'Stop it!' I screamed. I hardly recognised my own voice, pitched high, and thin, and frightened.

But in response they looked at me, and then at each other. Simultaneously they broke into easy jogs and headed towards the side of the property where a high wire fence separated the yard from the street.

I made to chase them, thinking that I would snare them in a chain-link net.

But when I turned the corner of the building I saw both men dip through a neat rectangular hole which had been cut in the fence.

I got to the hole in time to hear a car speeding away. I

didn't even see the tail lights.

I walked back to look at the storage bays. I didn't get close because I was barefoot but I was plenty close enough to cast my shadow on the whitecaps of broken glass reflecting the floodlights on the blacktop. I couldn't think why anyone would shoot up a stock of plate glass.

I walked back into the office and called the police.

I got my bathrobe and slippers and sat, waiting and trying to relax.

A patrolman arrived about fifteen minutes later, at about three-thirty.

We walked around the yard.

'What a fucking mess,' he said. 'Sheer fucking vandalism.'

The spread of the destruction in the broken glass made me sure that the rifles the two men had carried were broad pattern shotguns.

Albert Connah arrived at about the same time as the sector sergeant, a little before four. I heard the cars pull up and I went out to find them both looking at the hole in the wire fence.

Albert looked shocked and pale, the sergeant wiry and alert.

'I suppose you are Samson,' the sergeant said as I approached.

'That's right.'

'Some watchman. They must have been cutting this for fifteen minutes.'

'I'm a pretty heavy sleeper,' I said.

He seemed not to like that and he scowled. 'Wait inside, Samson,' he said. 'While Mr Connah and I have a look at the damage.'

*

When Glass Albert and the sergeant came in I was sitting at my desk with a can of beer.

The sergeant, whose name was Wisman, was offended. 'You're taking this pretty calmly.'

'I don't see much to be gained by rolling on the floor and pounding my fists.'

He seemed not to like that either. Then he looked at me as if struggling with a memory. 'Were you on TV the other day?'

'Yeah.'

'Christ,' he said.

There is no pleasing some people.

Wisman asked, 'Do you know the people who did this?'

'No,' I said.

'Were they friends of yours? Is that why they were able to do all that damage before you decided to poke your nose out of doors?'

This time I offended Wisman by saying nothing.

'I asked you a question, buster,' Wisman said. He moved close to where I was sitting. It was a threat.

'No, you didn't,' I said. 'What you did was to make an unfounded accusation in question form.'

I don't think he liked that either, but I was saved farther savaging when the patrolman who had surveyed the wreckage with me entered from the yard. He tracked fragments of glass in over the floor and he said, 'I found a couple of the fucking shot casings.'

He passed them to Wisman who glanced at them. He turned to Glass Albert who had stood unaccustomedly mute through the proceedings and passed the casings to him.

'What about it, Mr Connah?' Wisman said. 'You have this kind of enemy? What's life in the glass business like?'

Albert said shakily, 'I try not to step on people's toes.'

'Is there any point in somebody doing this? Is there

advantage to anybody? Does it do you any harm? Does it help somebody else?'

Albert thought. He shook his head. 'I don't see any point at all.'

Wisman turned back to me. 'Well?'

'Well what?'

'Could the shoot-up out back be somebody trying to cause trouble for you?'

I shrugged. 'Nobody comes to mind,' I said.

Wisman returned to Albert Connah. 'I don't like this guy's attitude, Mr Connah. I don't know whether it's just that he's done a lousy job of looking after your glass and isn't sorry about it or whether it's something else. If I was you, I'd fire him for sure.'

'I'll think about it,' Albert said.

'You do that. Meantime, I'll file a report and if anybody gets any ideas why this happened, you call in tomorrow.'

Wisman and the patrolman left.

Glass Albert stayed for a quick beer, but we were both too tired and too confused to say much. Before he left I asked, 'You going to fire me then?'

'Not tonight,' he said, but there was nothing of the usual vitality or bonhomie about him.

FIFTEEN

I woke up before eight, but lay in bed for a while thinking.

At nine I called the Belters. Douglas Belter answered and when I identified myself he said, 'Oh.'

'I'm sorry to bother you,' I said.

'That's all right,' he said. 'I should have contacted you. But life here is still rather confused.'

'I can understand that,' I said.

'You have things you want to talk about.' It was a statement.

'I think I have identified your wife's biological mother.'

'Daisy Wines?' he said, as if it were already known.

'That turns out to have been a stage name.'

'Oh.'

'I think I know her real name and some of her background. I can also make a guess why she left Paula with Mrs Murchison.'

'Oh,' he said.

'However, some of the information is not very pleasant and in the circumstances maybe it's not the right time for me to go through it. I am continuing to follow the leads which have been thrown up and, as much as anything, I'm calling to let you know that I am making a little progress.'

Belter thought for a few moments. He said, 'Come out, Mr Samson. Paula is taking everything pretty well and there will be no real advantage to spinning the shocks out, if shocks are what you have. Tamae has been a source of strength for her, as usual, and I am staying at home today. Frankly the thing that is upsetting her most is that the police have requested an autopsy. We hadn't expected that and it is delaying the funeral.'

'An autopsy doesn't usually take very long,' I said.

'The police have said that we will have to put a cremation off until their lab test results have come back. It may be as much as a week. Until that's all over, there will be no chance of an even keel here.'

'I'm sorry to hear that,' I said, 'but it's probably just routine.'

When I arrived the door was opened for me by Paula Belter. 'Hello,' she said.

'Hello.'

She smiled, formally. 'Doug says you have some things to tell us.'

'Yes.'

'Come in. Come in.'

She led me to the kitchen. She said, 'The kitchen seems to be the centre of action during the morning in this house. I don't quite know why, now that the boys are away so much.'

Douglas Belter came in from another part of the house as I sat on a comfortable, padded, straight-backed chair. 'Ah, Mr Samson. Would you care for a drink, or is this a little too early for you?'

'It's a lot too early for me,' I said. 'Unless we're talking about something like coffee.'

'Don't be disappointed, Douggy,' Paula Belter said playfully.

Douglas Belter frowned. I felt he was struggling to contain an explanation that if one of them were likely to hit the bottle at ten in the morning it was her and not him.

127

Loyalty beat self-defence. He said nothing.

'So, coffee it is.' Paula Belter went behind a kitchen bar to a U-shaped surface littered with appliances. After a moment standing still, she came out again. 'Tamae will do it. I'd like her to be here anyway.' She left the room. Belter sat at the table.

'You see how she is,' he said.

Something must have been clearer to him than to me, but I said, 'Yes.' Then, 'Mrs Murchison's death must have come as quite a shock.'

'Paula and Tamae went in to see her in the morning. Then by evening she was gone.'

'Did they ask her any of the difficult questions, about Daisy Wines?'

'Paula says not. But that doesn't exclude the possibility that she said something like, "We've hired a private detective to track down my real mother," as if in passing. Realistically speaking, I don't know whether the subject was raised or not.'

'We could ask Tamae, perhaps?'

'Perhaps.'

Paula Belter and Tamae returned to the room and Mrs Belter was saying, '. . . and I completely forgot where the coffee was. Would you mind terribly making it?'

'No, of course not.'

Paula Belter came back and started to sit at the table. But before she landed she rose again and went to a sideboard and took out four woven mats. 'Will we need utensils?' she asked, but as if to herself. Then to me she said, 'How about something to eat? Bacon and eggs? A croissant?'

'Nothing, thanks.'

'You're no fun at all, are you, Mr Samson?' She exchanged the mats for four coasters which she put on the table. Then, from a cupboard, she took four large mugs and put them on the coasters.

'Well, I've done my bit,' she said, 'and I'm absolutely exhausted.' She exaggerated a fatigued drop into the chair she had almost used a few moments before. Then she straightened and said to me, 'Not really. I'm just joking.'

I nodded. I said, 'I was very sorry to hear about Mrs Murchison.'

'Mmmm. So was I. She was like a mother to me, you know.'

'I think you're going too far, Paula,' Belter snapped.

'Oh, do you?' she asked lightly. To me she said, 'You know the police have delayed the funeral?'

'Your husband told me. I'm sure it's just routine.'

'Do you think so?'

'Since she died unexpectedly.'

'I thought that it might be because they thought she committed suicide.'

'Is that what you think?'

'It might be what *they* think.' She wagged her head. 'I don't know what *I* think.'

'Did she ever talk about taking her own life?'

'No,' Paula Belter said.

Tamae Mitsuki brought a pot of coffee to the table and filled the four mugs. 'Do you like cream or sugar, Mr Samson?' she asked.

'No, thank you.'

'I'll have both today,' Paula Belter said.

We all watched while cream and sugar were brought to the table and Paula Belter put a lot of each into her coffee. She sipped from her mug without stirring.

Tamae sat down, and Mrs Belter said, 'Well, Mr Samson, the floor is yours. Or should I say table?'

I was tiring of Paula Belter's self-indulgent stranglehold on group attention as a means of making sure no one forgot her suffering. There was no way to go in but hard.

'When I saw you last I had found a birth certificate which strongly suggested that your biological mother was named Daisy Wines. Later you remembered a woman called Auntie Vee who visited you at Mrs Murchison's.'

'Yes.'

'Well, I have learned that Daisy Wines was the stage name of a nightclub singer named Vera Wert who married a man named George Bennett Raymond Edwards. After less than two years she shot him dead in some sort of domestic fight. She was tried for his murder, but was acquitted in 1940. Immediately after her acquittal she left Indianapolis and . . .'

'Wait a minute, wait a minute,' Douglas Belter said. 'You're saying this woman was Paula's mother?'

'Yes.'

'For everyone's sake, let's take things a little more slowly.'

Paula Belter said nothing. She just sat with her jaw loose, as if the puppeteer were out to lunch.

I took them through what I had been doing and what I had found and I went on to a tentative reconstruction. 'She came to Indianapolis from Logansport in late 1935 or early 1936 when she was fifteen or sixteen. I don't know whether Vera Wert was pregnant when she came to town or whether she became so soon after. Either way, before the birth she found a singing job and obtained her new name. One could speculate that she was pregnant when she came to Indianapolis. That might be a reason for her to leave home.'

'The pregnancy?' Douglas Belter asked rigidly.

'Produced Mrs Belter.'

We all looked at Paula Belter, but she sat, quiet and grave.

I said, 'Vera, as Daisy Wines, was considered to be an

innocent. Her singing style projected it, and while she was being courted by the man she later married, she took no gifts from him and, it seems, gave none either. It may well be that around the club nobody knew that she had a child. One woman, who knew her slightly, wondered whether she would know how.'

'It's not something that takes a lot of knowledge,' Tamae suggested, suddenly breaking her silence when no one else spoke as I paused.

'That's true,' I said. 'Eventually, in 1938, she married Edwards. I don't know what she felt for him, but there is little question that his people presumed that her motives were mercenary. He was the wild scion of a significant family in this city. It could not have been easy for her, whatever it was for him. His sister remains convinced that Vera murdered him for the money and still manages to take pleasure in the fact that she didn't inherit as much as she might have. Nevertheless, as Mrs Edwards Vera came into a substantial amount. And my guess is that from that money she funded your upbringing, Mrs Belter. Her husband bought the New York Street property which the Murchisons ran as a boarding house the same year he married her, surely no coincidence. And I assume she was the source of the money to buy the house you lived in on 42nd Street and to pay for things like your piano lessons. I don't see where Ella Murchison came by it otherwise. Vera Wert may not have been around Indianapolis to visit you after the trial finished in 1940, but I strongly suspect that her influence and interest in your life remained for a long time.'

Paula Belter sat cupping the mug of sweet white coffee in her hands. Her glossy defences were gone. She looked sober and introspective and haunted and needful.

Having lost one mother so abruptly and finally, I felt that she would have given a lot to meet her other mother at that moment.

131

SIXTEEN

I said, 'The problem with weaving a reconstruction from a string of facts is that more holes are left than fabric. Maybe we have some of the main strands now. But a lot of questions and directions remain.'

Near to tears, Paula Belter put down her coffee. 'Whatever else happens, at least now I know she cared.' She dropped her face into her cupped hands, but she made no sound.

Then Douglas Belter coughed and asked, 'What additional lines of inquiry are you thinking of, Mr Samson? Whether she was actually guilty of murder?'

Paula Belter looked up.

'I had in mind Vera Wert's background in Logansport. Where she went when she left Indianapolis. Whether she is alive now and if so where. What happened to her. And whether we might find out who Mrs Belter's biological father was.'

I paused. Nobody filled the silence.

I said, 'But maybe you don't want me to go on. You hired me in the first place to get Mrs Belter a passport. That should be possible now, at least if you involve a lawyer to put it to the passport people in the right kind of way.'

'I see,' Belter said.

'And, the potential this kind of inquiry has for absorbing

132

money is very great indeed. The trail is old and cold and there is no certainty of any further success.'

Douglas Belter looked at his wife.

She became weary before us. 'You decide, Doug.' She rose slowly. Tamae helped her and the two women left the kitchen.

Belter and I looked after them, then at each other.

He said, 'She can be the most wonderful woman in the world.'

In a moment we heard a piano being played in a nearby room.

'A little emotional,' Belter said, 'but wonderful.'

I could see how his life would never be dull and that is a wonder of one sort.

Tamae came back into the kitchen and sat at the table. 'She'll be all right. It's just hard for her,' she said. 'So many surprises.'

We both nodded.

To Belter she said, 'Have you decided whether Mr Samson is to continue digging into the past?'

'I don't think there is much choice.'

She thought. 'I suppose not,' she said. Then to me, 'Do you have any other information for us now?'

'Only a picture.'

Tamae swallowed. Belter took deep breaths.

I took Charlie Carson's photograph of Daisy Wines, George Edwards, Mike Carson, Ginny Tonic and a third couple and showed it to them.

'Which one?' Belter asked haltingly.

I pointed out Daisy Wines.

'She looks so young,' Tamae Mitsuki said.

I was back in my office by eleven-thirty. That was the time Albert Connah had arranged to meet the insurance representative for an inspection of the damage.

133

They arrived together and we looked the place over. First the yard and the perpetrators' escape route. In the daylight we found some tyre burn trails which might have been made by the car they left in. I didn't remember hearing a squeal, but I could have been deaf to anything but the too fresh sound of breaking glass.

The insurance adjuster talked to me alone, but not for long and with no complications. Then he rejoined Glass Albert for a detailed stock-taking and they no longer needed me except for some form filling.

It meant I finally had time to face my unfinished business with Normal Bates.

I called him and said, 'I want to come and see you.'

'Does this mean you have freed yourself from your other client, Mr Samson?'

'No.'

'I see. You recall that I want you to start immediately?'

'Yes.'

'But you won't?'

'I am not able to, Mr Bates.'

'In that case, I'm not clear what it is that we have to talk about.'

'I have some questions to ask you,' I said.

'Have you?' he said quietly, even tiredly, and without stress on the interrogative. 'When did you have in mind?'

'I thought I would come over now,' I said.

'Why didn't you tell me you were a private detective?'

I'd taken my usual chair. Bates sat before his vast window scanning the city.

'You didn't ask,' he said.

'What kind of reason is that?'

He didn't answer the question, but he turned to face me. He said, 'You can't see the Marott Hotel from here.'

'What?'

134

'The Marott Hotel. The poor bastard. George Marott made his money in shoes and then he built the hotel. First major hotel north of White River. You know it?'

I knew it, but I said nothing.

'Huge place, and when it was finished Marott laid on big opening festivities. A hot dog with the works. Except . . . .'

He paused. I waited.

'Except,' he continued, 'that it opened in 1927. You've heard of the Depression, Mr Samson? Within a few years Marott was turning on lights in empty rooms so that people would think that somebody was staying there.'

Bates made a despairing exhalation that sounded like 'chew' drawn out. 'That's the way things were, and there was nothing that Reggie Sullivan or F.D.R. or Paul V. McNutt could do about it.'

Sullivan was mayor and McNutt governor in the thirties.

'What are you trying to tell me, Mr Bates?'

'That circumstances can make things different from how they appear,' he said sharply. For a moment his eyes and manner burst into life, but then he faded again. He was notably less positive, less definite, than when I'd visited him before.

But I was getting annoyed with digression.

'The George Bennett Raymond Edwards murder trial,' I said.

'What about it?' Bates asked matter-of-factly, as if he spoke of it every day.

'The woman my other clients hired me to search for is Mrs Vera Edwards.'

He seemed surprised. But he said nothing in response.

'I found out yesterday that you testified.'

'That's true,' he said. He closed his eyes for a moment. 'I did.'

'Will you tell me about it?'

He didn't speak immediately. I thought he was going to

135

say 'no', but he said, 'I followed her for a few months. I worked for an agency then. Apart from hole-in-the-wall outfits like yours, there were only two agencies in Indianapolis. Mine and the Pinkertons.'

'The Horse Thief Detective Association?'

He raised his eyebrows. 'Nowadays to look in the Yellow Pages you'd think people have nothing else to do but hire P.I.s. Fifty-three entries in there, last count. Fifty-three, including yours.' He shook his head.

'Mrs Edwards' husband hired you?'

'He thought she was screwing somebody on the side. I hated the job after the first couple of weeks. It's bad enough following someone every day when you have the sense that you only need to be patient to learn something. But when nothing happens, and days become months. . . .'

'When were you on the case?'

'Spring of 1940. I kept making negative reports and they kept telling me to stay at it. I began to think that at least I would get a summer at Maxinkuckee out of it, but then she went and shot him in April.'

'Maxinkuckee?'

'The gentry,' Bates said, 'used to send their womenfolk away for the summer. Either to select lakeland areas in Indiana like Maxinkuckee or Wawasee, or farther north, in Michigan, Petosky or Harbor Springs.'

'Oh.'

'It was meant to be good detective country. Husbands in the city at work, lonely wives far away. Personally, I preferred cases with more meat on them, but most P.I. work then concerned errant spouses. You had to do it. Couldn't make a living otherwise.'

'Tell me about Mrs Edwards,' I said, trying to keep him on my point.

'There's not much to tell,' he said slowly. 'She lived the life of the well-to-do ladies of the time.'

'That's it?'

'Yes.'

'All right. What was the husband like?'

'Totally obsessed with whatever he wanted at the moment, until he got it.'

'I've been told that originally he wanted Daisy Wines very badly.'

After a hesitation Bates said, 'Daisy Wines. Was that the name she used as a singer?'

'Yes,' I said, 'and according to you, by the time Edwards hired you he was trying to get rid of her.'

'Edwards wanted the goods on her. I don't think he ever said what he was going to do with them.'

'But even though you followed her all that time, you didn't come up with anything?'

'No.'

'Why didn't he go to someone else?'

Bates shrugged. 'I think my boss convinced him that if anybody could catch her at it, I could.'

'So Edwards still thought there was something to catch?'

'I gather he had no doubt at all.'

'Can I talk to your boss at Horse Thief?'

'Long dead,' Bates said quietly. 'I took orders, did my work, wrote my reports and turned them in. It was a good outfit as they went. Honest, because they were making money. I left in 1942 to go into the Navy. Spent the War as an M.P., first in Norfolk and then in Long Beach. When I got out I thought about going back to agency work, but set up on my own, here.' He pointed to the window.

'So you can't tell me about Edwards?'

'I only met him a couple of times. But I can tell you he was a nutcase,' Normal Bates said.

'What do you mean?'

'I mean he had a warped mind and it came out clearly at the trial and that's why his wife walked. Nobody who heard

137

her testify would have convicted her.'

'What kind of warped?'

Bates leaned back, breathing hard because he was involved in what he was talking about despite all the years.

'It's fashionable now for the rich to be sado-masochists,' he said. 'But to hear it described in a court of law in Indianapolis, Indiana, in 1940, detailed, was almost more than those of us who were there could bear. If Edwards hadn't been dead already, I think there would have been a man or two in the courtroom who would have made it happen by the end of that day.'

'Edwards' sister tried to shoot Mrs Edwards after the acquittal.'

'Small calibre from too far away,' Bates said dismissively.

We sat quiet for a long time.

I found myself thinking about the fact that he had plied my trade before me.

Perhaps we shared a wavelength. He said, 'The kind of life I've led, I ought to be dead.'

I said nothing.

'Are you reopening the Edwards case?'

'I have one main interest.'

'Which is?'

'Where she is now if she's alive. And if not, what happened to her. The Edwards trial is the most recent information I have, so far.'

I paused, but he didn't take the opportunity to volunteer anything more.

'She left town after she was acquitted,' I said. 'Do you have any idea of where she went?'

He looked quizzical. 'Me?'

'It must have been an important part of your life then, with the trial and everything. You might have heard something.'

'I never heard anything,' he said, hard now. 'As far as you could tell by me Mrs Edwards passed from the face of the earth a couple of days after it was over.'

I was restless when I left Normal Bates, but I didn't feel like simmering on it to work out why. There was a lot to do.

I stopped at a phone booth and called Miller. For a change he was not at his desk.

I checked my watch. Lunchtime. Wendy Winslow?

Lunchtime was about the earliest that there was a good chance of catching Maude Simmons in her office. I called. Better luck.

'I've just left a message on your answering machine,' she said. 'Did you get it?'

'No. I'm out.'

'You should have remote access. Well, if you can stop by, I have your trial transcript.'

I stopped by.

It was a hefty volume.

'Not as bad as if it were for one of the big money, society trials they have these days,' Maude said. 'It would be four times as thick. I suppose it's to help the people in the gallery who are writing books.'

I asked, 'Anything else?'

'Isn't that enough to keep you busy?'

'I wondered about a lead in Logansport.'

'Not yet.' Then, 'I have a meeting this afternoon with Kenny Gay.'

I brought the name back. 'The lawyer at Barker, McKay and Gay.'

'A senior partner,' she said. 'But no promises.'

I took the transcript home, thinking I would have a quiet read over a hamburger and oven fries. But I checked my answering machine first. Apart from Maude's call there was one other, from Miller. His message was, 'Get your ass down here, now.'

He still wasn't at his desk. But the reception officer at Homicide and Robbery with Violence, Sergeant Mable, knew I was expected and told me to wait.

My stomach snarled, but I sat. I read my transcript for twenty minutes.

Miller barely acknowledged me when he came into the reception area. He just said, 'Come on.' The way he said it left me with the feeling that he was a real policeman.

'Sit down,' he said when we got to his cubby hole.

I did; so did he.

He said, 'I don't want any gobbledy garbage from you, Al. Just a simple answer. I want to know how the hell you knew that Ella Murchison was murdered.'

SEVENTEEN

'The pathologist found a needle mark on her left arm. Her medical records didn't show any injections recently, and there was a little light bruising on her arms and on her abdomen, so he checked her blood. He found nembutal. It's an anaesthetic. And it's also used by vets. Somebody came in and put the old lady down, Al. The pathologist thinks whoever it was sat on her, maybe put a pillow over her face, and injected her.'

'Why inject her instead of suffocate her?'

'How the hell do I know?' Miller asked angrily. 'Maybe because suffocation is pretty easy to notice and he – or she – thought there was a better chance of nobody suspecting foul play this way. Which is damn well how it would have been, except for you.'

I tried to explain why I had felt suspicious.

'So all you admit to was the coincidence of her dying suddenly when she knew things you wanted to know and didn't want to talk about them.'

'That's all there was, Jerry.'

'What kind of things did she know?'

'I have been trying to trace a woman whose baby Mrs Murchison raised as her own daughter. The fact the child wasn't actually hers came out only a few days ago. Mrs Murchison was the obvious and best source of information about what had happened and about the woman who was the real mother. But she wasn't talking, either because she

141

was not clear-headed, or, more likely, because she didn't want to.'

'So who is this real mother and where do I find her?'

'I can tell you where she was in 1940,' I said.

When I left Miller, I went to a phone book and found the main office number for Douglas Belter's bank. But when I called his secretary said that he was at home. I called his home. It took twenty rings for an answer, but when it came the voice was Belter's.

I said that I wanted to come and see him. He agreed and didn't ask what it was about.

Belter answered the door himself too. He looked grimmer and greyer than ever, haunted, as if the accumulating shocks were getting near the too-much point. Maybe I was projecting my ideas of what a banker's life should be like, assuming that he wanted calm and organisation. Maybe he was really a night rover, pocket poet and garden revolutionary. But whatever way he cut his path, it seemed to be getting near the quick.

'Paula is in bed,' he said. 'Tamae is out.'

I followed him into the house and he led me to the kitchen. We sat at the kitchen table. He said, 'You said you were at Police Headquarters. Were you there about Ella?'

'Yes,' I said. 'They wanted to know if I knew who had murdered her.'

'Murdered,' Belter said. He held his head. 'My God!'

His shock was in finding himself in that sordid part of the world where human beings deprive other human beings of the miracle of life. It's not the sort of thing that actually happens, not to real people.

Except, sometimes, it does.

'There's no chance that . . . it could be anything else?'

'No.'

142

'How . . . ?'

'Somebody gave her a shot of an anaesthetic called nembutal. Somebody put her to sleep.'

He blinked. 'I've just had a call from a lieutenant named Miller. But he didn't tell me. . . .' His voice faded.

Miller must have wanted to see for himself how the news was taken. The lover of Wendy Winslow seemed far away.

'I know Miller,' I said.

'He said that he would come out this afternoon. He told me and my wife to stay at home.'

I sat and watched him stare at the table top for a few minutes.

'Mr Belter, did you kill Mrs Murchison?'

He lifted his eyes to me slowly. 'Did I what?'

'Lieutenant Miller will ask you that.'

With more time to prepare indignation he would have given a more vigorous answer than he did.

'No,' he said.

'O.K.,' I said. 'But here's another one.'

'Yes?'

'Your wife and housekeeper visited Mrs Murchison the morning of the day she died.'

'Yes.'

'Did either of them go back in the afternoon?'

'I . . . don't know.' Belter sat silently.

'Can I talk to your wife?'

'I would prefer that you didn't disturb her.'

'When is Tamae going to be back?'

'She shouldn't be long,' he said. As he said it, we heard the front door.

'I would like to talk to her.'

'All right,' he said, and he rose and left me in the kitchen.

A minute later Tamae Mitsuki joined me. She looked old and pale and small. 'Doug just told me,' she said. 'He's gone to look at Paula. He may call the doctor. He says the

143

police are coming here.'

'If she's not in a fit state to be interrogated, a doctor here to say so would be useful.'

'I don't know,' she said, which was comment on Mrs Belter's state of fitness, though Mrs Mitsuki looked none too steady herself.

'How much of Mrs Belter's moodiness is controllable, Mrs Mitsuki?'

'I don't know. I just do what I can to help.'

'You and Mrs Belter visited Mrs Murchison the morning of the day she died.'

'Yes. We did.'

'Did either of you return in the afternoon?'

Behind me a loud voice said, 'Why don't you just out and ask whether Tamae and I killed her, Mr Samson?'

As I turned, I saw Paula Belter, an apparition in a long plain white nightdress, standing in the doorway. Behind her, Douglas Belter seemed a shadow. I heard him saying faintly, 'Now, Paula.'

'It's not my job to investigate Mrs Murchison's death.'

'It's nice to hear that you remember what you're being paid so well for,' Paula Belter said.

'But the police will want to know and you should be prepared for their questions.'

'I think Tamae and I will manage to answer any questions which the police feel they need to ask.'

Tamae Mitsuki rose from the table and went to Mrs Belter. She said quietly, 'Mr Samson has more experience of police matters than we do. Perhaps he can help.'

Paula Belter shook her head. 'I want him to go. I want him to leave,' she said. She stepped forward. 'I want you to leave now. Leave!'

I left.

As I drove back down Meridian towards town, I considered

that Paula Belter had a reasonable point. I was hired to try to establish history and location of Vera Wert Daisy Wines Edwards. Whether Mrs Murchison's death arose from the investigation or not was irrelevant to the terms of my employment.

But I felt involved. I felt sure that the killing had some direct connection with developments in the case. But how they could lead to this murder I didn't understand. Paula Belter's real mother protecting the secret of her identity? But how would she know it was in danger? No, for the life of me, I couldn't think of a good reason why someone would want Ella Murchison dead.

Which only served to underline how much I didn't know. Because somewhere there was someone who had had sufficient reason, good or not.

EIGHTEEN

At Biarritz House I was told that Connie Howard was in the staff lounge talking to the polic. I gatecrashed.

Miller and a plain-clothes detective I didn't know were in the room with her. Miller looked distinctly annoyed when he heard someone coming in but when he saw it was me, he said only, 'The bad penny.'

Mrs Howard said, 'That is the man who came to my apartment. Before then it hadn't occurred to me that something might be wrong about Ella dying. But the more I thought about it, the less right it was.'

'You said that Mrs Murchison was behaving strangely,' Miller said.

'Only that several of her visitors said she was having memory trouble, but when I talked to her, she was fine. All the attention seemed to stimulate her. I felt she was as alert as she had been since I knew her.'

Miller sighed. 'The daughter and housekeeper were her only visitors that day?'

'Yes,' Mrs Howard said.

'Did she have any enemies among the other patients, or people that she feuded with, or people who envied her or disliked her for some reason?'

'There are always little tiffs, but there was nothing in the slightest way serious.'

'I see,' Miller said.

I said, 'When you say there were only the two visitors, in

the morning, does that include other residents stopping in?'

'No, no,' Mrs Howard said, 'We don't monitor in-house visits.'

'Or,' Miller said, 'the number of stops in her room by members of the Biarritz staff?'

Connie Howard looked at Miller sternly, a mother on the verge of scolding a child for being stupid and wasting time.

But hypodermic syringes aren't available only on the streets. Some doctors and nurses have access to them too, so Miller was being sharp, not silly.

He said, 'Did you see Mrs Belter and Mrs Mitsuki when they came that day?'

'Yes.'

'Did they have a bag with them, or any kind of package?'

'Not that I recall.'

'How long did they stay?'

'I don't really remember. Half an hour?'

'Were they together in the room with her all the time?'

'I . . .' she began. 'As a matter of fact, Mrs Belter did come out a couple of minutes before . . . ?'

'Mrs Mitsuki,' I said.

'She asked at the desk whether the doctor was on the premises.'

'Why?' Miller said.

'I don't know.'

'Did she look upset?'

'I don't remember her looking upset.'

'And did she go back to the room then?'

'Yes, but they left, her and the housekeeper, almost right away.'

'Did you stop to see Mrs Murchison in the afternoon?'

'Not after lunch.'

'Did you see anybody at all outside her room after that?' I said.

'No.'

147

Miller said, 'Thank you, Mrs Howard. That will be all now.'

Connie Howard rose tentatively, but left the room without saying anything else.

I said, 'What all have you got?'

'I only started when the autopsy preliminary came back this morning. This is my first stop.'

Miller's detective colleague said, 'You want me to keep taking notes, Jer?'

'What? Oh. No.'

The man closed a notebook.

Miller turned back to me. 'I'm off to these people who hired you now. Want to come?'

'I think I'll give it a miss,' I said.

'O.K.,' he said without interest. He left with his note taker.

I wanted to talk to Paula Belter. But considering the tone accompanying my recent exit, I decided it would have to wait. Maybe some undeferential cop treatment by Miller would make her more receptive to the prospect of my gentle questionings.

Even if some of the questions I had weren't quite so gentle.

So I went back to my office.

I finished the transcript of the Vera Edwards trial over a couple of sandwiches and a beer.

Vera Edwards had come back to her home at ten o'clock on the 21st of April, 1940, a Saturday night. There, husband 'Benny' Edwards was waiting for her. A houseboy employed by the Edwards family testified that 'Mr Benny' had been drinking heavily and was in a terrible temper. Vera Edwards did not appear unusual as she came in, was modestly dressed, well behaved and polite. He said that she always treated the servants with courtesy, in contradistinction to her husband and the rest of his family. Of the family, Wanda Edwards and the senior Mr Edwards lived in the house at the time. The houseboy, a maid, a cook and a chauffeur/gardener also lived on the premises.

The houseboy testified that Mr Benny Edwards shook his wife physically as soon as she returned to the house, and that he had called her names – 'tramp' and 'bitch' – and then told the houseboy to 'get lost'. The houseboy did not leave them until Mrs Edwards also told him that he should go on to bed.

The houseboy did not go to bed, although he admitted Mr Edwards was often, even routinely, abusive to his wife in front of the servants. Instead he did chores in and around the kitchen and was still there when he heard the shots.

The last he had seen of Edwards alive was as he led his wife by the wrist through the hall towards the conservatory.

The fatal shots had been fired more than an hour later. The time was agreed by both the houseboy and a key prosecution witness, Wanda Edwards.

Miss Edwards testified to being awake when she heard the shots because, although she retired early, she often found it difficult to sleep. And on this occasion she knew her brother was upset. She had come immediately from her room, and she claimed that she had been the first person to get to the conservatory, although her bedroom was farther away than the kitchen.

Vera Edwards had been standing over her husband's body, pointing the gun at him. Vera Edwards had said, clearly, coldly and challengingly, 'Move now, you bastard,' and when she had seen Wanda Edwards enter, she had raised the gun and said, 'You want some too?' Miss Edwards also testified that none of her sister-in-law's clothing had been torn.

This evidence conflicted with that of Mrs Edwards and of the houseboy. According to the houseboy it was he who had been first on the scene and Miss Edwards had arrived as much as two minutes after him. Mrs Edwards was sitting, with her clothes ripped and seemingly shocked, and the gun was on the floor where it was later found by the police. He testified that neither woman had said anything to the other but that after a moment, Mrs Edwards had risen and said, 'I must telephone the police,' and that she had then done this. Miss Edwards had stood looking at the body of her brother.

The first policeman had arrived on the scene about half an hour after the call. None of the other servants had appeared in the room and eventually police went to wake them all. Old Mr Edwards was unwell and the police had been convinced not to wake him.

In short testimony each servant confirmed that Mr and Mrs Edwards did not get along, that Miss Edwards loathed her brother's wife and that they had been asleep when roused on the night.

Although Benny Edwards was often ill-tempered and had abusive moods, the suggestion that he might have been more so than usual was supported by the fact that earlier in the evening he had learned from the family doctor that his wife was pregnant.

The doctor testified that he had called at the Edwards house and asked to speak to Mrs Edwards. When he found that she was out, he had given his glad tidings to Mr Edwards.

The doctor was astonished to hear Edwards respond by shouting that 'it' couldn't be his.

Wanda Edwards testified that her brother had complained frequently of his wife's 'coldness' towards him, that he was fearful she was seeing other men and that she frequently insisted on going out alone. She conceded that the medical news had upset him, but denied that he had been out of control.

Mr Edwards' jealousy was confirmed by the head of the Horse Thief Detective Association. And by Normal Bates.

Bates, an agency operative, had followed Mrs Edwards for more than four months and he had followed her on the night of the death. She had gone to a concert at the Indiana Theater. He had followed her inside and she had spoken to no one. He had then followed her back home. She had travelled each way by taxi.

Normal Bates testified that in eighteen weeks of full-time surveillance he had seen nothing to suggest that Mrs Edwards was other than a faithful wife. He confirmed that she sometimes went places alone, but repeated that he had never seen anything which was in the slightest amiss.

The defence concluded with Vera Edwards' own testimony. In cross-examination she was harshly challenged about the paternity of her impending child, about her background and morality before marrying Bennett Edwards, about the reasons she married him. And about why her husband should be so quick and positive that a pregnancy had not been caused by him.

Vera Edwards seemed to attempt to answer the questions clearly and decorously, but some very direct questioning forced her into the descriptions of her husband's brutality and bestiality which had so incensed Normal Bates.

It was clear that the jury believed Mrs Edwards rather than Miss Edwards. Picturing the innocent girl-like figure I knew from Charlie Carson's snapshot, I found it easy to understand.

Nevertheless, the transcript added to the questions I wanted to ask in the Belter household. For one thing, about the 'coincidence' that the houseboy employed by the Edwards had been Japanese, and named Mitsuki.

NINETEEN

I called the Belters' house. Douglas Belter answered after many rings. He said that the police had only just arrived, that Paula was in bed, that the police were insisting on talking to her, that things were chaotic.

I told him I wanted to come out again, but that I would leave it until later. He hardly reacted.

Which left me at home, waiting.

I hate waiting when there are things I want to do. Killing time is worse than passing time. More like death.

But I was let off the hook. Maude Simmons called.

She sounded merry. I told her so.

'A little too much to drink at lunch, Albert my old fruit,' she said.

'I see.' I looked at my watch. 'This man Ken Gay isn't an old flame of yours by any chance?'

'Ask me no questions and I'll tell you no lies.' She giggled.

I have never heard her giggle before.

As if noting the break in her customary façade, she said, 'Which is more or less what he told me about your Vera Edwards.'

'What do you mean?'

'She must be very rich. They give her the full Howard Hughes treatment.'

'Come on, Maude. What are you saying?'

'He wouldn't tell me anything about her at all. Well,

that's not quite accurate. He confirmed that they represent the Vera Edwards estate and he said that any message we cared to formulate would be passed on to the appropriate party or parties.'

'He used the word "estate"?'

'Yes.'

'Doesn't that mean that she is dead?'

'He would neither confirm nor deny that conjecture.'

'Did he go back on the word "estate" as if it had been, maybe, more informative than he intended?'

'He said precisely what he meant to say. He's that kind of man. He said that estate is the word he had been instructed to use – by the estate.'

'Oh,' I said. 'I had hoped for more.'

'As the actress said to the circumcised bishop.'

I was silent.

'All work and no play,' Maude said. Then she took a breath and said, 'There is a little more.'

'Go on.'

'He said that there was no point in trying to extract information from lesser members of the firm, because they wouldn't know anything about this client or these clients. The records are off limits to everyone but partners and he prepares the correspondence himself.'

'Did you hint that approaches might be made to other people in the firm?'

'No. He knew that you asked about her yesterday morning and left a note. I don't think he rates the ethical standards common in your profession. He's warning you off sucking up to the secretaries.'

'So the note isn't going to get me anywhere.'

'He said it was being dealt with.'

'I see,' I said.

'The only other thing I have done is compile a list of people named Wert in Cass County.'

'O.K. Give me that,' I said. 'I have some time this afternoon and I'll make some telephone calls.'

She dictated the list. It wasn't very long.

Before dialling a series of strangers in the vicinity of Logansport, I called Charlie Carson's house.

'He ain't here. Who is it and what do you want?'

I gave my name and said it was about one of his old photographs. 'Is he at the club maybe?' I asked.

'It's about pictures?'

'Yes.'

'Well, maybe he just come through the door. I'll go see.'

Seeing didn't take long.

'I was out back,' Carson said. 'It's where I get away from business and I don't like to be disturbed by guys after money, that kind of thing.'

'And singers wanting auditions,' I said.

'Yeah,' he said. Then, 'You want to know if I've figured out who the third couple in that picture was, don't you?'

'Yes,' I said.

'Well, I ain't. I been through the books and there ain't nothing to cross reference on them. Sorry.'

'If it's not there, it's not there. But there was also another favour I wanted to ask.'

'Let's hear it.'

'I wondered if you might be able to reconstruct Daisy Wines' employment record during the years she worked for your father.'

'Yeah,' he said. 'I suppose I can do that.'

I said, 'In particular I'm looking for the first date you have on her. I'm trying to establish when she came to Indianapolis. So if there's anything before she actually worked, an audition or, anything, I'd appreciate it.'

'O.K.' Carson said cheerfully. 'I'll have a look.'

I offered more than gratitude.

He said, 'We'll see. So the picture is all right, huh?'

'It's in good shape,' I said. 'It meant I could show Daisy Wines' daughter what her mother looked like.'

'Ain't that something,' he said. I could visualise the huge man smiling. 'Well, ain't that something. Gladys will love that.'

A telephone straw poll showed conclusively that none of the three Logansport Werts who answered their telephones would admit to knowing anything about a distant female relative named Vera, last seen in the mid-1930s.

I worked hard on the phone, trying to establish how grateful I would be for information, photographs or leads of any kind. Grateful as in cash money.

It was a risky precedent, this offering of money for things. I could see how I might grow to like it. It certainly made people more eager to listen to me. I received three promises to think about Vera Wert and to ask other members of family about her. The full list of Werts had four names. One had not answered.

When I had finished I thought about the Belters again and began chewing my fingernails.

In the end, I just went.

I considered it possible that I would meet Miller and his entourage, but when I pulled into the spacious area in front of the garage, there were no other cars sitting in the light drizzle.

I gathered my notebook, prepared myself for the possibility of a steely reception and marched up to the doorbell. I punched it with great authority. It cried back at me that I could have been another Sugar Ray.

The door was answered by Tamae Mitsuki. She blinked a few times when she saw me. She said, 'Come in, Mr Samson.'

155

As I crossed the threshold, Paula Belter appeared in the hall asking, 'What is it, the return of the fuzz?'

'Hello, Mrs Belter.'

She put her hands on her hips. 'Doug is in bed. What do you think of that?'

'I'm pleased you're feeling well enough not to be fighting him for space,' I said.

Forcefully she said, 'I've been talking to the gentlemen of the police.'

'Lieutenant Miller?'

'Yes,' she said. 'You know him?'

'Yes.'

She looked at me. 'No hint of how, or where, or why? No undercurrent of hostility from days he took you in and roughed you up?'

I said, 'Our acquaintance preceded his choice of profession. I've known him from school days.'

'I see. The cameraderie of the less privileged classes.'

'How did you get on?'

'With your lieutenant and his sidekick? Like a house aflame. He was very polite and hardly even suggested that Tamae and I might have sneaked back into the Biarritz with loaded hypos hidden in our brassières.'

'He likes to take a soft approach before he arrests someone for murder,' I said.

She sighed. 'I know I'm being horrible. I'm being horrible, aren't I, Tamae?'

'Yes, Mrs Belter.'

'It is all such a strain. Do you think I could have a cup of camomile tea? That's supposed to calm one, isn't it? Would you like a beverage too, Mr Samson?'

'Thank you, no,' I said.

'I promise it won't be poisoned. And I'll answer any question you care to put. But maybe I am being presumptuous. Is it me that you wanted to talk to?'

'I would like to have a word with each of you,' I said.

'Each?'

'You, your husband, and Mrs Mitsuki.'

'Tamae, you've hit the big time. Questions of your very own.'

Mrs Mitsuki stood looking at her employer. 'Do be quiet, Mrs Belter,' she said. Turning to me, she asked, 'Are you sure you won't have a cup of tea or coffee?'

I said, 'I'll have a cup of camomile tea too, thank you.'

We adjourned to the kitchen. It seemed almost home territory to me now.

Tamae Mitsuki spent a few moments putting the tea and cups out and water on to boil but by the time I asked Mrs Belter my first question, Tamae was there to hear.

The question was, 'When, as exactly as you can recall it, did you last see the woman you knew as Auntie Vee?'

'Exactly? You mean the day?'

'If you can fix it.'

I expected a flippant remark, a home sarcasm, but Paula Belter closed her eyes and appeared to think and then said, 'I can see that green scarf. She had it around her hair before she went outside. It was windy and . . . and maybe it was raining. Or, am I guessing?'

'Was it day, or night? Had you seen her often before then or was it unusual?'

'It was day that time,' Paula Belter said. 'I don't know why but I remember it was—' She stopped suddenly. 'Good heavens.'

'What?'

'My dolls' house.'

'Your—?'

'I grew up with the most gorgeous dolls' house.' Her eyes showed the excitement and even the size of it. She spread her hands. 'It was huge.' She paused. 'It *is* huge. It's in the

157

attic now. I saved it, in case I had daughters, but I never did. We tried it on the boys, but they weren't interested.'

She fell silent again, and I waited.

She said, 'What I've remembered is that Auntie Vee gave it to me. A Christmas present. It was all wrapped up in white paper with thin red lines and gold balls and three stripey ribbons and bows and it was as big as I was. I couldn't believe it was for me when I saw it under the tree and. . . . And she was there when I unwrapped it.' Paula Belter shook her head slowly. 'I didn't remember until now. She was there.'

Paula Belter looked at me. Her voice was strong. She said, 'That wasn't, however, the last time I saw her, which is what you want to know. She brought things for the house. I remember tiny brass vases and plates and cups and saucers. Miniature cutlery. She brought things for it week after week. And we played with it. I remember a little Easter basket with tiny eggs.' She grew shrill. 'Oh God! How could I let my mind mislay all that? I played with those things for years!' With fists, Paula Belter beat her temples.

Mrs Mitsuki was impassive. Which eased the uncertainty I felt watching the woman beat herself. Shortly, Paula Belter stopped.

'The last visit,' she said again. 'I don't know exactly. I remember that she hadn't come for a while, and that when Mom called me I ran like hell because I hoped Auntie Vee would have something new for the dolls' house. But she didn't. She brought dresses instead. Six or seven or eight or . . . I don't know how many, but I remember she said to Mom, "And she'll need some for winter", and I thought that was peculiar because it wasn't winter. It wasn't even summer yet. But there were summer dresses too. I wore them when I started kindergarten. I remember that.'

'Can you work out which year that would have been?' I

asked.

There was a silent contemplation. '1940,' she said after a while. 'And Auntie Vee cried that day. I don't remember about what, but I can see her, dabbing her eyes with the ends of her scarf. I thought that was strange too, because she should have used a hanky.'

Mrs Mitsuki rose from the table and by doing so gave us relief from the intensity of Paula Belter's reminiscences. She poured boiling water into a small teapot and carried it on a tray back to the table. She stirred the contents of the pot and then poured a mild yellow liquid through a strainer into each of three cups.

Paula Belter said to me, 'I'm not always like this. Am I Tamae? Usually I'm quite steady, aren't I?'

'Yes, Mrs Belter,' Tamae Mitsuki said.

'All right, Mr Samson,' Paula Belter said sharply. 'What was it you wanted to ask Tamae?' Suddenly there was a twinkle in her tired eyes.

'I have another question for you,' I said.

'Oh, come on! Don't be so stuffy! I won't go away.' She sipped from the hot weak liquid. 'Don't be a party pooper!'

Mrs Mitsuki said, 'What is it that you wanted to know, Mr Samson?'

I acquiesced. I asked, 'Just how common a name is Mitsuki among the Japanese in this country?'

She looked at me for several seconds, before she said, 'It's not particularly common.'

'Mrs Belter's biological mother's household had a Japanese houseboy named Koichi Mitsuki.'

'My husband's name was Koichi,' Tamae Mitsuki said slowly.

Paula Belter's eyes opened as wide as strawberries. She put her tea on the table.

'Was he from Indianapolis?' I asked.

'I met him in Los Angeles,' Tamae said slowly. 'I knew

159

that he worked once for a family in Indianapolis, but he never told me about it.'

'That's surprising.'

'Why?'

'Because he was an important witness in the murder trial of Mrs Vera Edwards.'

'He only ever said there had been trouble which cost him his job, that he told the truth when his employers wanted lies, so he was fired. But he never told me the circumstances.'

'When did you meet him?'

'In August of 1940.'

'How long had he been in Los Angeles?'

'Not long. A few weeks. His brother was in business with an uncle of mine and he was invited by my parents to our house.'

'When did you marry?'

'September 20th, 1940.'

My face asked, 'So soon?'

'It was love at first sight,' she said stonily.

'And what happened to him?'

'He is long dead,' Tamae Mitsuki said.

'I'm sorry.'

'Not a fraction as sorry as I am,' she said. 'He treated me like a human being. That is not a common thing between a man and a woman.'

'Do you remember any times when he had communications with someone who might have been his former employer?'

'No,' she said.

'Or from anybody who might have known him in Indianapolis?'

She shook her head. 'No.'

'What sort of work did your husband do in Los Angeles?'

'He was not able to get domestic work without a letter of

160

reference. He helped in his brother's grocery business for a while. But less than fifteen months after we were married it was Pearl Harbor.' She looked at me. 'Do you know what happened to the Japanese who lived on the West Coast after Pearl Harbor?'

'They were interned, weren't they?'

'Rounded up. Dispossessed. Herded into camps. Over a hundred thousand people, the first within two months of Pearl Harbor. And not just Japanese subjects, but naturalised and native-born Americans too.'

'I'm sorry,' I said lamely.

'Koichi died in there. Manzano. That was the name of our camp.'

'You were imprisoned too, Tamae?' Paula Belter asked.

'Not at first, but soon.' She shrugged. 'Not content with that, they encouraged the men to sign up for the army. They had a special unit, all Japanese American. I wouldn't let Koichi go. We had our son by then. But Koichi died anyway.'

'How did he die?' I asked.

'Pneumonia,' she said. 'He was not hospitalised or treated. I have been told since that there could have been a law suit for neglect. But that was not the point.'

'No,' I said. Then, 'why did you come to Indianapolis?'

'My family, as the war drew to a close, and after, kept going on at me to marry again. I didn't want to, so I left. I came to Indianapolis because Koichi had worked here. It was almost the only other place in the country I knew the name of.'

'How did you meet Mrs Murchison?'

'She was the only boarding house proprietor who would give me a room.'

'So you stayed at the house on New York Street?'

'Yes. With my son. As a boarder at first, and then I did housework for her. But the property was in bad condition and was soon sold. Mrs Murchison invited us to come with her, but her new house was small. I kept my own place until Hiroshi left home.'

'Hiroshi is your son.'

'Yes. I still worked for Mrs Murchison and later for others and we got through.'

'You must have been very sorry when Mrs Murchison died.'

'She was a friend when no one else was,' Mrs Mitsuki said simply.

'Did Mrs Murchison ever talk to you about the woman who—'

'I have been here when you asked questions of Mrs Belter and her husband, Mr Samson. If I had any information which could have been of use to you, I would have said so. There was nothing. We did not talk a great deal. I am not a great one for talking.'

'All right,' I said. 'Thank you.'

We all used our teacups as punctuation, a pause, before I began again and said to Mrs Belter, 'My other question.'

'Oh.'

'When you visited Mrs Murchison the morning of the day she died . . .' I could see Paula Belter stiffen. 'You left Mrs Mitsuki with her and asked to see a doctor.'

'Yes.'

'What did you want a doctor for?'

Paula Belter played with her lips. She said, 'I was angry at her.'

'Who?'

'Mom. Mrs Murchison. I told her I was fed up with her refusing to answer the questions about my past. I told her I thought I was entitled to know and when she avoided answers I thought she was faking and that I was going to tell her doctor and that I was going to get him to help me, maybe give her truth serum.'

162

'I see,' I said. 'How did she react to that?'

'It upset her,' Paula Belter said. 'The poor old lady.' She took a deep breath. 'Not the way one would wish to say good-bye to someone who was one's mother.'

I was wading from one neck-deep emotional pond to another. I didn't mean to be insensitive but I was tiring of lachrymogenic tales and had things to sort out.

I asked, of them both, 'And the threats didn't produce any further information?'

'No, Mr Samson,' Tamae Mitsuki said sternly.

'All right,' I said. 'I want to speak to your husband, Mrs Belter.'

'Must you?'

'I suppose not but I have a suggestion that will involve a decision for you to make together. I can explain it for you to pass on to him when he feels better.'

'He feels all right. He's just tired. The doctor, *my* doctor, insisted that *he* go to bed.'

'Is this something about Mrs Murchison?' Tamae asked.

'No. It is a way to try to precipitate knowledge about Mrs Belter's mother.'

They both looked attentive.

'I have located someone who either knows where Vera Wert Edwards is or who knows what happened to her,' I said.

'Who?' Mrs Belter asked.

'A lawyer in town whose firm represents Mrs Edwards or her interests. What I suggest is that you consider legal action,' I said.

'What kind?' Mrs Belter asked.

'If your mother has died, then you have a claim on her estate. If they won't say that she is alive then they are obstructing the course of such a claim. The idea is something like a writ of *habeas corpus* to make the law firm produce your mother in a court. At worst, they'll prove she is dead. At best, you might get to meet her.'

163

TWENTY

I drove back to the centre of the city on Meridian Street. I
thought about a couple of visits I could make but stamped
them Immediate Attention, Tomorrow. I hardly glanced at
Wanda Edwards' house as I passed it.

It was half past seven by the time I crossed the bridge
over Fall Creek, near The Fandango, where I was not
keeping track of Lance Whisstock. But it made me think of
law and order. I stopped at a liquor store and bought a six-
pack.

I drove to Vermont Street and parked in front of a three-
storey frame house of turn-of-the-century vintage. There
was a glow through the curtains on the ground floor. I took
the six-pack and went to the front door. I rang the bell and
a porch light came on.

It was answered by a tired-looking man with thin grey
hair and only seven toes. 'Hello, Powder,' I said. Leroy
Powder was another lieutenant of my acquaintance in the
Indianapolis Police Force, head of Missing Persons. But to
call him a friend would be to take liberties with the word. It
is hard for those of us not privy to his innermost workings to
think how a social roughneck like Powder could actually
have a friend.

He sighed heavily. He said, 'If you hear one coming, you
leave by the back, which is why you people have to wear
gumshoes.'

164

He did not invite me in.

'Show some hospitality or fix the porch roof,' I said. 'It's wet out here. I even brought you some beer.' I held the six-pack up. 'I won't stay long enough to drink more than one.'

He stood mute before me for several seconds more. Then he made way and held the door. As I passed him he said, 'A gumshoe bearing gifts. Who did you kill?'

We sat in his front room. When I had been there last it was covered in papers like a snowfall. Tonight it was tidy, clean, even sparkling on the bits which could reasonably be made to sparkle.

I broke two cans off the pack.

Powder left the room. He returned with two glasses. He put one down next to me, and picked up one of the beers.

'And lost weight too,' I said. 'Someone is having a good influence on you.'

He opened the can, filled his glass and drank. 'O.K., shamus,' he said. 'I've accepted your bribe. What is it that you want? The answer is no.'

'I came on an impulse,' I said.

'Strange urges you P.I.'s get.'

'I'm trying to trace a woman who left Indianapolis in 1940. I don't know where she went or for sure whether she is still alive now. Other things have happened, even a murder, but the core of the job is a Missing Persons case. I'm confused as hell, so I thought I would be humble and come to an expert.'

'Office hours begin at nine,' Powder said.

'Come on!' I said. 'I read all your PR in the papers about the best Missing Persons solution rate in the Midwest. I'm paying you a compliment. Help me.'

Powder sipped from his beer.

I drank mine quickly and felt the benefit.

I told him about the case.

165

'You don't know where she went in 1940?'

'No. No idea.'

'But she cares for this child.'

'Set her up with a woman as a mother. Provided money all through childhood.'

'What am I supposed to do for you, gumshoe? Pull the broad out of a top hat?'

'I don't know,' I said. 'Make a suggestion? Give an opinion?'

'I don't think your *habeas corpus* ploy will help you much.'

'I'm hoping to establish whether she is alive or dead.'

'In the fullness of the time it takes to utilise the law?'

I smiled, accepting the point.

'So what are you left with from the 1940 end?' Powder leaned back and rubbed his face with both hands. 'The dead man's sister,' he said. He thought. 'I suppose Miller could check out the houseboy in California for you.'

'Miller is pretty busy with the Murchison case, and some personal problems,' I said. Then, 'But why check that?'

'I don't like his wife coming back to Indianapolis. What's the name again?'

'Mitsuki.'

'Why the hell come here? There is no Japanese community here. There are a dozen other places she might have gone first.'

I thought about it. I said, 'I have the feeling that she was pretty unworldly then. Maybe even now. She still gets emotional about her husband, and that was more than thirty-five years ago.'

'A long time,' he agreed. 'But you asked.' He shrugged. 'Or you could try to go at it from the other end.'

'What do you mean?'

'If this Edwards woman cared about the kid,' he said, waving a finger at me, 'enough to arrange for her bringing-

166

up, then chances are she still keeps some kind of eye on it. If she's alive. Either she isn't far away or she has somebody here who lets her know how the kid is doing.'

I paused with a lip on the rim. I said, 'That makes considerable sense.'

'I always make sense,' Powder said. He looked at his watch. 'Go away, will you?'

On the way home I stopped at a supermarket and filled a recycled paper bag with an ecologically unjustifiable steak. A thick one.

For a change there was no message on the answering machine.

I was grateful, because my mind was in tired tatters.

I grilled my steak: 'Where were you on the night of November 18th?'

I was sopping up the last of the blood with instant mashed potato when the telephone rang.

I felt better for the food. I answered immediately.

It was Charlie Carson. He said, 'I got a date for you on that Daisy Wines thing.'

'Good man.'

'She first worked here August 11, 1935. She did two weeks. I don't know if you know the business . . . ?'

'No.'

'It's a slow time, August. He hardly paid her anything. A kind of audition rate, you know. But she musta been O.K., because she did two more weeks at the beginning of September and she got better money. There was two more weeks in October, nothing till end of February in '36, and then it was off and on until June. June she started a long spell, five straight months. One of the regulars, Ginny, you met her, yeah? She went away for a while and Daisy Wines got herself established. Her money went up good. Ginny got back December. That's when the newspaper shot I showed you was took. The picture you got is from early '38.'

'I'm very grateful that you've taken the time to look all this up.'

'No problem. Makes a nice change from kicking the tails of fourteen-year-olds who think they look like they're twenty-one.'

He agreed to accept more than my thanks, when I returned his photo. We hung up.

I sat by the phone and thumbed through my notebook.

Paula Wines Belter had been born February 5th, 1936. Making conception sometime after the beginning of May the previous year. When her mother was sixteen. Within a couple of weeks of Paula's birth, Daisy Wines was working again.

I fidgeted.

The accretion of information about Daisy Wines was making me restless. Every time I learned something, more questions flaked up.

After pacing around the room, until the mice that live under my floorboards began banging their ceiling with pieces of stale cheese, I decided to call my woman friend and maybe go out. She would understand.

'You're not in a fit state to be with anybody,' she said within a minute on the phone. 'You always get like this when some case is not resolving itself. It addles your brain. Why take it out on me?'

She understood only too well.

I hung up in a moment of isolation and despair.

But then, as it sometimes does, the telephone relented, and rang.

'Hello, love.'

A light thin female voice with a thick rural accent asked, 'Is that Mr Samson?'

Addled or not I sensed a need to speak gently. 'Yes Ma'am, it is.'

'Are you the one that's offering that there reward for information rendered about Vera Wert?'

'I am certainly trying to learn more about her, yes.'

'Could you tell me how much in the way of payment that might be, please?'

'It depends really on how good the information is.'

'Well, it couldn't hardly be none better,' she said.

'Why's that?'

''Cause I'm the only sister what she's got, and the onliest living direct close relation because all our brothers is dead.' This was said with strength and defiance.

'Can I know your name, please?'

'I am Miss Winnie Jane Wert.'

'Where are you, Miss Wert?'

'I have me a little house in Peru.' In Hoosierland we pronounce the town Peé-roo.

'I know it's late,' I said, 'but would you be willing to talk to me about your sister tonight?'

'That would suit me just fine,' she said.

I looked at my watch. Nine-twenty. 'I would think that I could be there a little before eleven.'

'I'll be here,' she said.

I asked for and received instructions for getting to her house.

'Would you,' she asked, 'be bringing cash money?'

'I can do that,' I said.

'You ain't never said how much you was thinking of.'

'Would twenty dollars be worth some of your time?'

'I was thinking more like . . .' She thought. 'Twenty-five?'

Miss Wert's house was a clapboard shack on the edge of Peru on the Wawpecong road. I made good time, even at

169

55 mph, on US 31, a divided highway all the way to Nead. From there it was another five miles. I pulled up outside the house at two minutes past eleven.

There was no bell so I knocked at the door. A dog round the back barked a couple of times and some paint came off on my knuckles. After a minute, a short, round woman with one burn-scarred cheek opened the door a crack.

She asked, 'Who's there?'

I gave my name and she stepped back to invite me into a room which was Spartanly tidy.

'Make yourself at home,' Winnie Jane Wert said. She was dressed in a loose gingham dress with vertical stripes. It looked clean and recently ironed.

I sat and before she followed suit she said, 'I hope you got cash money.'

'Yes,' I said.

'Because I ain't got no cheque account. Don't cotton to banks a lot.' She sat down and faced me.

'You looking to capture Vera for something, or what?'

'I'm a private detective,' I said, 'and I'm just trying to find out what happened to her and where she is if she's still alive.'

'Someone say she died?' Miss Wert asked, with her dark eyebrows arching under mostly grey hair. She seemed to be in her mid-fifties.

'No. But I don't know much about her since about 1940, and it's a long time.'

'She sure left these parts since a long time,' she echoed. She shook her head, looked down and sucked her lower lip. 'My big sister,' she said. 'My onliest big sister.'

'When did you last see her?'

'*See* her? When I was seven years of age.'

'Oh.'

'That was in 1935, two years after Ma and Pa was took.'

'Took?'

170

'Died. They was at a bank, in Logansport, and some robbers come in. They was a sheriff with his deputy come along and gunplay opened up and Ma and Pa both got theyselves killed. Trying to get out'n the line of fire of the one bunch they ran in front of the other. Both of 'em had their heads blowed off.'

'How many children were there?'

'The six of us. Vera was the old un. Earl was next, then Cloyd. Me, Jimmie Luke and baby Emmett.'

'What happened to you all?'

'Too many to stay together. The two youngest went to Pa's brother. That was his son's wife you called on the telephone today what then called me and give your number. Me and Cloyd come to a friend of Ma's here in Peru. Earl and Vera got placed with different folks in Logansport so as they could be near to go to school there. The deal was they would help at the houses.'

'Who did Vera get placed with?'

'Doctor and Mrs Wingfield, only she runned away. Took off and nobody ain't seen her since. I didn't see her since they got us together Easter time. The Wingfields was real nice people and saw us kids right as far as meeting up a couple of times a year was concerned even after she left them. But the last time I saw Vera was Easter in 1935. By time the Fourth of July rolled around she was long gone from their house.'

'Do you know why she left?'

'Not real for sure,' Winnie Wert said. 'But she did take me aside and have a talk about staying away from mens. I was only seven, but I recall that clear. She talked to me because I was her real sister, onliest one she got. And I'll tell you straight, I sure wish I had listened to her better.'

'So you think she had trouble from a man here?'

'I didn't know nothing about it at the time, but I could guess who that was.'

'Who?'

'Tommy Wingfield.'

'The doctor?'

Winnie Jane Wert laughed hard. 'Gracious me, no. Old Doc Wingfield was a sweet, kind, gentle kind of man. This was his boy, his only boy what lived in the house with 'em. He must of been eighteen, nineteen when Vera was there and I know for a fact that he made a lot of little babies in his day.'

'Does he live locally now?'

She grew momentarily grave. 'No. He don't live at all. He got killed in France in the War.'

'I see,' I said. 'And that's the last you know of Vera? When you saw her in 1935?'

Looking at me sharply the woman said, 'Now, I didn't say that, now did I? That was the last time I *saw* Vera, but I heard from her since then. Plenty.'

'When?' I asked, my heart starting to race.

'Oh, lots of times.'

'When was the last?'

'The last? Lessee.' She looked at me. 'You know that all the boys, each an' ever one, is gone.' Then, in case it wasn't clear, she added, 'Dead.'

'All your brothers? I'm sorry to hear that.'

'Last was Earl. That's ironical, ain't it, him being the oldest. But he passed over from cancer, it was three years ago come March.'

I sat.

'Sad time it was. He had him four kids and a wife. Hard on them.'

'And you heard from Vera then?'

'Not direct, to me. But she sent a wreath and five hundred dollars for the family.'

'Three years ago?'

'That's right. And she's had her a wreath at ever single

172

funeral. Each of the boys. And she made a gift to the families too.'

'But she didn't attend any of the funerals?'

'No, sir.'

'Why was that?'

'I'm sure I don't know. Maybe she was too far away to come.'

'But who told her that the boys had died?'

'I don't know that neither. She just knowed. And more than that, she knowed other things. She knowed when I was down on my luck and she got me . . .' Miss Wert paused. 'I got to say, I was in jail for thieving, which I did only because I was real hard up and not because I'm a bad person. But Vera give me money, a kind of allowance, when I come out. It ain't enough to live high on, but it keeps me going. Pays the rent on this place, even if the landlord lets it get like a pigsty outside.'

'How did you start receiving this allowance?'

'Governor of the reformatory had me brought in and told me how my sister had contacted them and set it up. Give me a speech on taking advantage of the opportunity.'

'How do you receive the money, Miss Wert?'

'In cash. In hard cash. I get me a letter that I got to sign for, twice ever month.' She spread her hands, palms up, resting on her knees. 'Like I say, it don't go very far and when I got extra expenses, you know. . . .'

I nodded. 'Where are the letters mailed from?'

'They come from Indianapolis. But they won't help you much.'

'Why not?'

'The address is some lawyers, and you know lawyers.' She winked. 'Well, maybe you don't know 'em, but I never had no joy from no lawyers. And these that sends the money, I wrote to them last year when I was sick and I had some time, see, and expenses, you know. It was a letter of thank you to send on to Vera, but I didn't get no comeback. Wasn't just no cold neither. Pneumonia I had. But nothing. So don't talk to me about no lawyers.'

'Is there anything else about Vera?' I asked.

'You ain't saying that you knew everthing I already told you?'

'No. You've helped a lot.'

She sank back on her chair with visible relief. 'Oh, that's good.' After a moment she said, 'I don't really know nothing else. I got a picture though. That any good?'

Before I answered, she rose and went to another room. She was gone only a moment and returned with a small photograph. 'This is it.'

It showed the Wert family, all eight of them, in a posed snapshot taken outside a house. The youngest child was in its mother's arms, and Vera Wert was easily identifiable as a slight, serious-looking girl, standing stiffly next to her father, a sallow-faced man with tiny eyes and stubble visible on his chin.

'I would very much like to borrow this, if you would let me.'

She shook her head. 'Oh no.' Then she stopped shaking her head. 'But I'll sell it to you for . . . ten bucks?'

TWENTY-ONE

Friday dawned wet and cold. I woke with the light, but ruminated for a long time in bed before getting up. I charged it as work time.

I often do my best work in bed.

I cooked a big breakfast. I washed all the dishes. At nine-thirty I went to the phone.

I called the police department, got put straight through.

'Lieutenant Miller.' The voice was strong.

'You sound like a razor-keen ambitious cop again,' I said.

'I feel reborn,' he said.

'I'm pleased for you, Jerry. I'm pleased you're getting some joy.'

'I have no idea where it's going to lead, Al. But we are good for each other. I kind of keep her feet on the ground and she kind of keeps my head in the air. Food even tastes better to me now.'

'And you're not resigning?'

'No. We're looking to keep the status quo, on the surface.'

'So, no TV slot?'

'It's been shelved. I'm an unofficial consultant. It wouldn't be the right career move for me to change jobs now.'

I could visualise him smiling. Then he asked, 'What did

you want?'

'An up-date on the Murchison case.'

'Nothing new,' he said.

'Nobody's remembered anyone going in or out of the room?'

'No. We've covered all the staff on duty and most of the residents. There is a lot of routine traffic in the corridor so somebody probably did see but didn't notice. We're trying a reconstruction, as many people repeating their movements as possible.'

'No feelings about whether or not it was someone to do with the nursing home?'

'We've got no evidence about anything yet, Al.'

'Good luck,' I said.

I went out into the big world. My first visit was to the house of Wanda Edwards.

I rang the bell three times before the door was answered by bestseller-writer-in-the-making Jane Smith. She wore a long quilted dressing gown and her puffy face said, 'If you think I look rough on the outside, just be thankful you aren't participating in what's on the inside.'

'Yeah?' she said aloud.

I asked to see Miss Edwards.

She said, 'Hang on,' and closed the door.

It took so long for her to come back that even a patient person like me was on the verge of having a go at the bell again.

But then the door reopened. 'You didn't tell me who you are,' Jane Smith said.

'You didn't give me the chance.'

She sighed deeply. 'Jesus. Hell. Shit. Come in.'

When it's put right, I don't need asking twice.

'I was here a couple of days ago,' I said.

She looked at me, but as if the effort hurt her eyes. 'I

don't remember,' she said. 'So who are you?'

I told her. Then I said, as we walked into the depths of the house, 'Feeling the effects of a bit of late research?'

She stopped, turned and spoke, each action completed before the next began. 'Were you part of the scene last night?'

'No.'

'What do you know about my research?'

'Virtually nothing,' I said. 'We established that fact the last time I was here.'

'Oh.'

She turned, led with her right foot and followed it with a left.

We stopped outside the conservatory door. I told her my name again, without being asked.

She looked at me with a painful squint of recollection. 'A detective?'

'Yes.'

'You guys sure pick your times.' She entered the room, closing the door behind her.

I looked at my watch. It was a little after ten.

Jane Smith reappeared almost immediately. She passed me without a word, and I took that to be an invitation to enter the room.

Miss Edwards sat in a chair by the wall of windows which faced the rear garden. I walked towards her and she turned to face me. She placed the palms of her hands together and touched the joined tops of her index fingers to the point of her chin. It was an attitude of serious contemplation.

'Mr Samson,' she said. 'The private investigator.'

'May I sit down, Miss Edwards?'

'Certainly.' She didn't point, but there was a choice of three wicker-framed cushioned chairs.

I sat.

Miss Edwards said, 'I have been thinking about death. Something that someone of my age has good reason to take into account.' She paused, but not long enough to force me to make the social sound of hoping earnestly that she see us all out. The old woman looked slighter than I remembered, but purposeful. She said, 'Do you know that I am the last surviving member of my family? That when I die the line will end?'

'I didn't know that,' I said.

She smiled slightly over the tops of her fingers. She said, 'Oh, I think you did.'

'I suspected it,' I said, 'but, in fact, it is a closely related subject that I wanted to speak to you about.'

'I see,' she said. 'I see.'

'I meant to work up to it more gently.'

'That is candid of you. Say what you must.'

'I have been reading a transcript of your sister-in-law's trial.'

What smile there was vanished.

'Please tell me to go if you are not willing to talk to me about it.'

Her hands dropped to rest one on each leg. She took a deep breath. 'You reopened all that for me the other day,' she said. 'Ask what you want.'

'My key question is to do with your testimony that your brother was positive he was not the father of the child which his wife was expecting.'

'Yes,' she said.

'Miss Edwards, what I need to know is how he could be so sure, and how you could be so certain that he was sure.'

'I knew my brother, Mr Samson. I was present when he received the news. His reaction was immediate, instinctive and true. It was surprise, shock, and anger. I had no doubt then and have no doubt now. Benny would know. He said it couldn't be. So that is the fact of the matter.'

I said quietly, 'You realise it would mean you have a niece or nephew somewhere.'

'There is no chance whatever of that being the case,' Miss Edwards said.

'All right.'

She leaned back. 'The things that woman said.'

She meant Vera Edwards in her testimony about Benny's sexual predilections.

'I hadn't thought about it for decades.' She looked beyond me, somewhere distant. Into the past? But it was only for a moment.

She said, 'I realised I knew very little about my secretary yesterday. So I asked her what sort of books she wants to write.'

'I see,' I said.

'They are so smart, these young people. But so misdirected. Life was so positive, so organised and orderly when I was a young woman, a younger woman. I long for those days.'

'What do you miss?'

Her hands found each other once again and then palm slid past palm so each set of fingers gripped a wrist. 'Myself, I loved the shopping. We had real stores then, where the clerks knew you by name and made you feel as if a customer was something worth being. Hasson's, Lieber's, Charlie Meyer's for buying presents and Ayres of course.' She tilted her head and remembered. 'You could get fresh fish easily. It was something to do with the railroad connections from the east, but we had such lovely oysters and lobsters and fish.'

I watched her become younger with the pleasure of remembering.

'And there were concerts. I used to go to the Murat for the symphony. When it was hot they opened the doors. No air conditioning then. And it meant you'd get unscored bells from the street cars as they went up and down outside.'

She stopped talking abruptly and her face grew harder and she said, 'Of course *she* had no appreciation of real music.'

'She?'

'But what do you expect of a night-club whore? Why Benny had to take up with her is something I never, never, never understood. So many nice girls.'

I said, 'What parts of her life as your brother's wife did your sister-in-law take to?'

'None.' Arch, sharp and short.

'Not the parties?'

'None of our people would invite them.'

'The home organising?'

'Nothing. A quiet, resentful slut. Not an ounce of feeling for my brother. And he was a boy who needed someone to care for him. The only thing she did for poor Benny was to sing to soothe him sometimes. I would hear her thin little voice wailing out some base tune or another. A siren's call. She lured him to the very rocks and destroyed him.'

I was allowed to find my own way out. But instead of doing so I spent a few minutes wandering around the house.

I found Jane Smith in the dining room. She sat in a haze of pot smoke, holding her breath and a cigarette. In front of her, making a condensation ring on the table, was a glass of orange juice.

'Miss Edwards asked that I remind you to use coasters under your glasses,' I said, 'and to be careful about ashes on the carpet.'

Jane Smith looked up blearily. 'What? Oh. Yeah.'

She sat still.

There was a buffet behind her. I tried some drawers and came across some place mats. I took one and put her glass

180

on it. I dried the ring with my jacket sleeve and left the ashes to fate.

She looked at me and said, 'I remember you now.'

'The cloud lifting with the hair of the dog?'

She grimaced.

I said, 'I want to ask you a question.'

She shrugged.

I sat in a chair next to her and said, 'As you went into the room to speak to Miss Edwards you said, "You guys sure pick your times".'

'Yeah.'

'What did you mean by "you guys"?'

'I meant you private-eye guys.'

'Has there been another private detective here?'

'Yeah. Nice looking too, if you like the executive type that carries a calculator instead of a gun.' She hesitated. 'Do you carry a gun?'

'Three.'

She looked impressed. 'Can I hold one?'

'I only take them out when I'm going to shoot someone,' I said.

'Oh.'

She drew, then sipped.

'I don't know what you said to Miss Edwards the other day, but she's been a different person.'

'Different how?'

'She's been active. And she's been talking to me. She told me this weird story about her brother being murdered. She's even gone out of the house for no special reason a couple of times. When she's gone out before you wouldn't believe the production number it's been.'

'And she hired a detective.'

'Yeah.'

'He came here this morning?'

'No, no. Day before yesterday. But it was late for

181

business, you know. After ten p.m. I kind of had some friends in.'

'Are you sure the man was a private detective? As opposed to a police detective?'

'Miss Edwards had me look them up in the Yellow Pages and give her the name of what looked like the biggest. The guy's card said he was from them.'

'Which agency was it?'

'National Security Company.'

'Do you remember his name?'

'Roger something. Look, what's this about? You going to detect the detective now?'

'Miss Edwards does not have a high opinion of private investigators. It's interesting that she has hired one herself.'

Jane Smith didn't share my interest.

I got up. 'How's the book coming?' I asked.

She looked at me. 'That meant to be some obscure double entendre or something?'

I left quietly.

TWENTY-TWO

I made my way south to Tarkington Tower.

It would have been sensible to stop to call Normal Bates and warn him I was coming. To confirm he was there. To let him wash his breakfast dishes and vacuum and clear his overnight popsy from the premises. I even had the dime.

But I just didn't feel like it.

I buzzed from the lobby.

Within a few seconds he called down on the intercom.

I told him it was me.

'Who?'

I repeated my name.

And then nothing happened.

After half a minute by the clock I buzzed again.

He said, 'What do you want?'

'To talk,' I said.

'Wait,' he said.

I stood for more than five minutes. Finally the voice through the speaker said, 'Are you still there, Samson?'

'Yes.'

He buzzed the door release. I entered the lobby.

No one had come out while I was waiting. I called both elevators. When they reached the ground floor, both were empty.

I used the stairs to get to the twelfth floor. I didn't pass

183

anybody coming down.

So maybe he used the five minutes to make a phone call.

Bates opened the door for me. He looked mountainous as his belly spread red braces. His smile grew only as he saw I was breathing heavily. 'Meet anyone interesting?'

'The elevators are out of order,' I said. 'You should report them.'

The smile finished its short life and was replaced by something rockier. 'So what do you want?'

'Do I get to come in?'

He led me into his sitting room. He sank into his rotating upholstery and left me to use my initiative on the straight-backed chair at his computer table.

Instead of moving the chair I felt the keyboard unit, the disk drive and the monitor. They felt cold.

'They feel warm. What you been up to?'

He said nothing. The bright eyes watched me closely.

I sat down. 'How do I get information out of this thing?'

He didn't answer for several seconds. I began to try switches.

'Stop that,' he said. Then one by one he told me which switches to throw and what keys to hit.

When we got as far as 'Talk to me, baby,' I typed, 'Lance Whisstock' and hit the 'enter' key.

The monitor screen filled with the information which I had printed a copy of on my first visit to Bates' apartment.

'How do I clear the screen?'

'Hit "execute," then "k" for clear.'

When I was ready to start again, I typed 'Albert Samson' and entered it.

I was rewarded with a screenful of details. All the personal facts one could think of including my reported net income for the last six years and my current bank balance.

At the bottom it said 'Space Bar to continue.'

The continuation listed the names associated with the

important cases I've worked on over the years and my 'known friends'.

A third visual 'page' gave a 'Personal Evaluation', including an IQ and comments on my reliability, honesty and personality.

I read everything carefully. It represented an impressive piece of research, of private detection.

When I turned to face Bates, he was gazing at the city through that wonderful window.

I said, 'My daughter has moved. How do I correct her address?'

He swivelled slowly to face me.

'She lives in Austria now.'

He took me through the procedure. I put in Samantha's current address.

'You going to harass me some more by having goons shoot her place up too?' I asked. 'What do I type to make that happen?'

'I don't know what you're talking about,' he said sharply. He also looked puzzled. Maybe I was wrong about that, but I wasn't wrong about other things.

'Why have you got all this stuff on me, Mr Bates?'

'I'm writing my memoirs.'

I nodded agreeably. I turned back to the machine where I cleared the monitor of my life story and then typed and entered 'Vera Wert.'

The screen read, 'No listing.'

I tried 'Daisy Wines,' 'Vera Edwards,' 'Mrs George Raymond Bennett Edwards.'

No listing for any of them.

Without looking at Bates I said, 'Come on! Tell me how I access the data on your biggest case.'

'Turn it off, Samson.'

Obligingly I turned the computer off. I moved my chair close to his. I sat, faced him, and leaned forward. 'Maybe

185

you remember everything about the Edwards case so clearly you can write it straight off for your memoirs.'

'I'm tired,' he said. 'I want you to leave.'

'If I do, I'll be replaced by cops questioning you about a murder investigation.'

'You keep talking in riddles,' he said. 'If you won't leave, then please tell me what it is that you want.'

'To talk.'

'So talk.'

'O.K. I feel like talking about your testimony in the Edwards murder trial.'

He didn't speak.

'Mrs Vera Edwards. Tried for the murder of her husband. We are agreed that you are the Normal Bates, private investigator, who stated under oath that he had followed her for four months?'

'I told you about that before,' he said.

'You told me Mrs Edwards didn't do anything which suggested she was being unfaithful.'

'That's right.'

'Let's talk about that. For instance, you testified that the night of the shooting Mrs Edwards took a taxi to a concert at the Indiana Theater, didn't talk to anybody while she was there, and took a taxi home.'

He said nothing.

I said, 'But Mrs Edwards didn't like concerts. And even if she went to this one, there was no reason for her to go by taxi when the family employed a chauffeur and none of the other members of the family was out of the house that night. Comment?'

Bates said nothing.

'Seems to me,' I said, 'that if she travels by taxi, it can only be because she doesn't want anybody in the household to know where she's going. There's no one easily available to confirm where she went. Except you. Am I bringing it all

186

back?'

To my utter astonishment I saw tears begin to form in the old man's eyes. He lifted his hands to his face, and he whirled away from me to face his window, his city. Wet snow, not heavy, was falling.

I stopped talking. I had more to say, but little by way of hard facts. Mostly inconsistencies as I tried to join up the things I'd been told. But I also had my anger, from being used and lied to, and from having been gullible.

Almost as abruptly as he had turned away he moved his chair to face me again. With a voice which hardly betrayed recent exposure of emotion he said, 'You, of all people, know what a mean job this is.'

'This?'

'Don't be obtuse. Private investigation.' He shook his head. 'For our working lives we do routine or boring or dubious or dirty jobs on behalf of people with problems they mostly create for themselves. The pleasure in it is the occasional success of proving one person is a cheater or thief and we sell the news to another cheater or thief. I know men in this business who spent twenty years with the idea that a good case was one where the people they were taking pictures of didn't punch them on the nose. Maybe some guys get women flinging their bodies at them day after day. Maybe some guys get a lot of genuinely interesting jobs. Maybe you're one of them. But I wasn't. I only once got a case where there was a beautiful woman who didn't look at me like I was a piece of shit.'

He breathed heavily a few times and coughed. The coughing grew violent and the vast stomach rocked. I worried that the man might be dying before my eyes.

'Are you all right?'

By way of an answer, he grew still. He said, 'I followed her, like I said, long hours. She wasn't stupid and knew her husband was looking for an excuse to dump her. So she

187

took precautions when she went out. Circuitous routes. Changing means of transportation. But she wasn't hard to follow for a pro and I stayed with her all the way on her first visit.'

'This was to the house on New York Street?'

'Yeah. Murchison's.'

'So why didn't you report it?'

'I'm not finished,' he said venomously.

'Sorry.'

'The target goes into the house. But that's not what my client wants to know, not just that. He wants to know what she's doing in there and who she's doing it with.'

He stopped to scratch his forehead, hard.

'So I see her go in and I decide to have a look around. A sign in the window says there are rooms to let, and it looks like an ordinary rooming house. She could be visiting anyone. I walk around the place to see what I can see. Only I get caught.'

'Caught?'

'Earl Murchison. Mrs Murchison's husband. I walked into him. I was careless, too pleased with having trapped the target so quickly.'

'I understand.'

'So after a little toing and froing about who I am, what I'm doing and do I want the cops or fist in the face, I let him take me inside. I think maybe with a little money I can get him to help me out and I'll have the case wrapped up with a bonus in record time.'

'And?'

'And we go into the living room and instead of a private chat about which boarder's room Mrs Edwards has gone to, there is the target herself. She's shooting the breeze with Ella Murchison and playing with a little kid.'

'I see.'

Normal Bates closed his eyes. 'Samson, she was the most

beautiful thing there was. I'd never seen anyone like her, not up close. She had a natural presence, carriage, yet when she talked it was just like real people. Not snobby. Just people.'

He sat for some moments before he opened his eyes and faced the world again. Me.

He said, 'I might have tried to hide what I was except I had already told too much of the truth to Earl. So I played it straight. And in return, they played it straight with me.'

'Which was?'

'The little girl was Vera's from before she met her husband, who didn't know anything about the kid. She only married Edwards to guarantee the little girl's security.'

He paused.

'That was it?' I asked.

'No. She told me about her husband. That he was crazy. That she tried her best for him, to keep up her side of the deal but that he kept changing the rules and that the Murchisons and her daughter were her only refuge.'

I sat and watched while he worked himself up to continue.

He said, 'That night after we talked, I drove her home. I hadn't agreed to anything. There had been no offer to me although it was clear that they wanted me not to report what I'd learned to her husband. On the way home we didn't say anything about the situation. We just talked about where we grew up. Radio shows. Little stuff. Friendly stuff.'

He pointed a finger at me. 'I'm telling you, Samson, I was a cut above the others. Most of the guys in our job then were trash. Greedy and heartless and with no feelings for human beings. I was better than them. I had position, but I didn't take advantage.'

Quietly I guessed, 'So she took you to bed.'

He said, 'The only time in my life.' He remembered, but briefly. 'But it wasn't a trade-off. It may look like it. It may sound like it. But it wasn't. For one thing, it didn't happen until after I had already made two weekly reports to her husband. For another it was her idea. No, not idea, because . . . well, it was in my head from the first minute I was in the room with her. But she was the one who said it. She said, "I want to go to bed with you," right up, like that. I couldn't believe it. I was so surprised that all I could say was, "Thank you."'

'It doesn't sound like such a bad thing to say,' I said.

'Only happened four times,' Bates said, but he said it as if it put him four ahead of the rest of humanity.

But however much I might respect the way he treasured the memory, delicacy was not what I was there for.

'And in return, you perjured yourself,' I said.

'It wasn't like that. I did my job. I followed her exactly as I said I did. We rarely met. And I saw nothing at all which suggested that she was unfaithful to her husband.'

'Except with you. You thought your client would accept the distinction?'

He looked at me, disgusted that I could try to sully the thing which was, perhaps, the most beautiful in his life.

'And the child she was pregnant with in April, 1940, was yours,' I said.

'No,' Normal Bates said.

I looked surprised.

'Not mine.' He was quiet but definitive.

'How can you be so sure?'

'She was sure. That was enough.'

'Whose was it then?'

'Her husband's,' Normal Bates said.

I didn't like that. My face showed it. '*I'm* pretty sure,' I said, 'that the child wasn't her husband's.'

'Then you're wrong,' he said.

'I don't understand your certainty.'

'These things are calculable.'

'When was the child born?' I asked.

'I don't know,' he said.

I didn't like that either.

I said, 'Why not?'

'I never saw or heard from her again. After the trial.'

I spent a full minute doodling in my notebook. I asked, 'Did you ever marry, Mr Bates?'

'Not for any practical purposes.'

'What does that mean?'

'I eloped with a girl I knew in high school when we were both seventeen. Her parents and my father knocked sense into us by not separating us. It only lasted two years.'

'Any kids?'

'No.'

'Never tempted to marry again?'

'Not marry,' he said.

'But you've participated in meaningful relationships?'

'One or two,' he said.

'And,' I said, 'a woman you adore, who might be pregnant with your child, walks out of your life one day and you settle for never seeing or hearing from her again?'

'It wasn't a question of settling for it. She left. I didn't know where she had gone.'

'A capable private detective,' I said.

'I looked for her. I tried to find her,' he said.

I said, 'I don't believe you.'

'An intelligent woman with money can get lost, Samson. You ought to know that.'

'It takes time and planning. When was she sorting it all out? In the spare hours between sessions in court? Saying to herself, just in case I get off I will do this and that and thus, so I can vanish from sight within a couple of days?'

He shrugged.

'Like hell you don't know. Someone who can't shake a tail is not going to succeed in leaving a city where she's notorious, without anybody noticing. No way. You obviously helped her, Mr Bates. You probably worked it all out for her.'

'I deny that,' he said.

'Just like you got her off in court.'

'Now just—'

'You tell me,' I said, with my finger pointing between his eyes, 'you tell me what the jury would have done to her if you had told them about the dutiful wife who kept a premarital child secret, who took her husband's private eye to bed. A wife who happened to be carrying a gun the night her husband happened to find out she was pregnant and he knew it couldn't be his. Just let me ask you this, Mr Bates. Did anybody at the time ask you where the hell you were the night of April 21st, 1940? And don't you think that somebody might have if they had known what you've just told me?'

My passion and feeling seemed to calm his, just as often someone being more afraid than you makes you braver. He sat with a faint smile on his face and when I had been quiet for a few moments he asked, 'Do you accuse all your clients of murder, or just the select few?'

'It's not a joke,' I said.

'I murdered nobody. Nor did I conspire to murder anybody. Nor did I conspire to assist Vera Edwards at her trial. No one asked me to do anything. What I did was my own idea. I expected nothing for doing it and I did it because it was the only way I could see of helping justice to be done.'

'Perjury?'

'Justice as I understood it when I took a hard look at my job and made a moral decision. Maybe you've never done that and don't understand it. I'm not even asking you to believe it. You have ferreted various things out and would have been left without accurate facts if I had kept silent. I've told you the truth now. So if you go the wrong way, it's your own responsibility.'

'And what is the right way to go, Mr Bates?'

'Just a manner of expression, Mr Samson.'

'The way I want to go is to find Vera Edwards.'

He shrugged. 'If she's still alive, you mean?'

'You say you don't know where she is?'

'First you insist that I knew where she went in 1940,' he said. 'Now it's knowing where she is today? Honestly, I cannot help you.'

'Whatever portion of your story I come to believe, Mr Bates, I believe least that your contact with Vera Edwards ended after the trial in 1940.'

He shrugged again.

'And it's not only that you wouldn't let her get out of your life that easily.'

'No?'

'Where do you get your money, Mr Bates?'

'What?'

'An apartment with a view like this is one of the priciest ways to live in Indianapolis. Where's the cash come from?'

'I worked hard for a long time,' he said.

TWENTY-THREE

As I got off the elevator I saw a tall young man in a suit that looked too good to take out of the box. He was outside the locked door studying the apartment list, but when he saw me, he moved to the door, waiting for me to come out.

I opened it but stood in the doorway. 'You don't live here,' I said suspiciously.

He hesitated, assessing me. Then he said, 'No, I've come to see a Mr Bates.'

'Normal Bates? The private eye?'

He smiled slightly. 'That's right. Do you know him?'

'I should say I do. Hey, you aren't a private eye too, are you?'

'I am, as a matter of fact,' he said.

'Jeez,' I said. 'That must be real interesting. Is it like it looks on the programmes and that?'

'I find it unfailingly fascinating,' he said.

'Gosh,' I said.

'Do you know Mr Bates well?' he asked.

'Oh, I have a lot of time for Mr Bates. A terrific kidder, he is.'

'Oh,' he said.

'And he's interested in computers too. But I bet you private eyes all know about computers these days. I bet you hardly ever have to go following anybody. You just put your computers on them, huh?'

'Computers can be very useful,' he said, beginning to

show impatience.

'Golly, its wonderful to be alive in this day and age, isn't it? That's what I tell Norm all the time and he agrees. Hey, I do envy you guys, doing the interesting jobs you do all the time and meeting all those girls. Is it easy work to get into?'

'Like everything these days,' he said, 'standards have risen out of sight.'

'Need to be a high school graduate now, huh? Not good enough any more to be an ex-boxer or cop?'

Uncertain of me he said, 'You need a college degree for an interview with a decent agency and you almost need a post-graduate degree to get hired. But please excuse me. If you don't mind, I'd like to go on up. O.K. if I come through?'

'Oh sure,' I said, moving and holding the door for him. 'You must be a real busy guy.' He passed me and walked to the elevator.

'Which apartment does Mr Bates occupy?'

'It's 1203,' I said. 'Just tell him you're a friend of Al's. Good luck with him, Roger,' I said and left the building quickly.

I went north again, to the Belters'.

I spent a long time at the door, ringing the bell a second and third time.

But I was in a determined frame of mind.

Finally, Tamae Mitsuki opened the door.

'Hello, Mrs Mitsuki,' I said.

Her eyes flickered over me for a moment, and then she said, 'I'm sorry, Mr and Mrs Belter are both out.'

'That's all right,' I said. 'I've come to see you.'

'I am just about to go out myself,' she said.

'I'll try to be concise and to-the-point.'

'I don't know if I can postpone my appointment.'

'It's important,' I said.

Inside the house, the telephone began to ring.

She maintained her guard at the open front door for only a moment. She made way for me, just as I had for Roger the Agency Op, and she retreated quickly to the telephone.

I followed.

She realised I was with her and passed one extension, heading for parts of the house I had not been in.

I picked up the telephone and said, 'Belter's residence.'

The party at the other end said nothing. I heard breathing and strained to hear the cogs and wheels whirring in the caller's mind. Finally a decision was arrived at. The party hung up.

I replaced the receiver as Mrs Mitsuki watched me impassively.

I said, 'I tried to sound like Mr Belter when he answers my calls. But maybe the caller expected Mr Belter to be at work and mine was the wrong voice answering. What do you think?'

She said, 'You seem to be making an effort to be obnoxious, Mr Samson. Why is that?'

'Because you have told me some lies, Mrs Mitsuki. And I'm in an extra-bad mood because you're not the only one who's been doing it.'

She opened her eyes wide and looked supremely innocent. 'Lies?'

We sat in the kitchen.

I said, 'I am now certain not only that Vera Wert Edwards is alive but that she has a regular source of information about her daughter.'

Mrs Mitsuki watched me.

'Nothing to say?'

'Should I have something to say?'

'Since you are the source of information, I would think that you would want me to congratulate me on finding out

196

the hard way what you could have told me easily.'

'That is ridiculous,' she said. 'I am not such an informant.'

'Oh, I think you are,' I said.

We looked at each other.

I said, 'There are a few touchstones which make the conclusion inescapable for me.'

'If you tell me what they are, perhaps I can explain where you've gone wrong,' she said. Cool.

'O.K. The first is a coincidence I don't like.'

'Which is?'

'The Belters originally came to me because of the dud birth certificate and my investigation then turned up Mrs Belter's connection with Vera Edwards. On the same day Mr Belter hired me, I was approached by a man who had been so involved with Vera Edwards that he committed perjury at her trial to help her get off. Two people with important connections to one woman. That is quite a coincidence.'

She shrugged.

'Not interested? Well, I am. Because I am sure now that I was hired by the second man so that he could keep an eye on me or even get me to drop the Belters' case, which he tried to do. But the point is this. To contact me so quickly – the same day – he had to know the Belters' plans and what the false birth certificate might lead me to. You are the only person apart from the Belters themselves who knew about the decision to hire me. And you would only know the significance of the birth certificate if you had regular contact with Vera Wert Edwards.'

I waited.

'Nothing to say, Mrs Mitsuki?'

After several seconds she said, 'I find your accusations extraordinary.'

'There is more to come,' I said. 'And worse.'

She sat impassively.

I read it as support for my contentions.

I said, 'Vera Edwards is out there somewhere. She is interested enough in her child not only to support her and Mrs Murchison through the girl's childhood, but to maintain you as an information source. Why, I ask myself, does the real mother not just appear, tell the story, and take a more direct part in her daughter's life?'

I paused. Nothing.

'Must be some good reason. Now, life's funny, full of far-fetched explanations for things. Mrs Edwards might have things in her life that she is too ashamed for her daughter to know. She might be married to a politician or some other kind of gangster. Or it could be that what she's hiding is worse than shame.'

I paused.

'It could be she feels guilty about having murdered her husband on April 21st, 1940, and doesn't think she could manage to talk people – her daughter – into believing she's innocent a second time. Just speculation, of course. But what do you think of it?'

Mrs Mitsuki maintained her silence. But suddenly I felt she was tired, that a hardness in her gaze was gone. I didn't know how close to the truth I was. But I felt some of my pot shots were hitting home. They had to be.

I said, 'Another question. How did Mrs Edwards make contact with you in the first place? I say you lied when you said your husband never heard from her. An association with her is the only plausible way to explain why you should choose to come to Indianapolis after the war, instead of staying put in an established Japanese community. And the fact that you just happened to find Mrs Murchison, who happened to be bringing up Mrs Edwards' daughter, wraps the package and puts a bow on it. Another coincidence?'

I said, 'I'm calling you a liar, Mrs Mitsuki. Are you not inclined to say something about that?'

Slowly she said, 'You said there was worse. Was that it?'

'No,' I said.

'Finish what you have to say.'

'There are two things. The first is that I suspect your late husband was at least an accessory in the murder of Mrs Edwards' husband.'

She breathed sharply.

But I was rolling. 'I've already found one man who lied for her at the trial. If your husband was treated well by Mrs Edwards, and hated Mr Edwards, it is likely that he would tailor his testimony of events to favour Mrs Edwards. His version of the events on the night of the shooting differs considerably from that of the dead man's sister, who claimed to be on the scene almost immediately after the shots. The jury accepted your husband's story. I wonder if they would now.'

'Koichi was a man of honour,' she said stiffly.

I followed a new tack. 'You and he married shortly after he arrived in Los Angeles, yes?'

'Yes.'

'On what money? You said he didn't have a secure job. Why did your family allow a rapid marriage to a man with uncertain ability to support his wife? Is that the way in the Japanese community?'

She glared at me.

'I think not. So I must conclude that he arrived in L.A. with a nest egg substantial enough to impress prospective in-laws. But where from? Did he save so much out of a servant's wages through the depression years?'

I saw her begin to speak, and it would have been with feeling. But she drew her lips, tight, swallowed, and said nothing.

'Which brings me to the extraordinary fact that Mrs

199

Murchison was murdered a few days ago. *Murdered*.' I exhibited the feeling now. 'Why should anyone kill an institutionalised woman in her eighties, of unreliable mental clarity?'

I paused again, though I had given up expecting answers to my questions from anyone but me.

'It is too much of a coincidence to think that her murder was not related to the recent revival of interest in Vera Edwards. So, looking for a motive we can ask, aren't Vera Edwards' secrets safer now that Mrs Murchison is dead? And if Vera Edwards was involved, we're entitled to ask, Mrs Mitsuki, what then might your involvement have been?'

She sat before me now breathing heavily.

I said, 'This woman has been responsible for the taking of two lives.'

'It's not so!' she said. The words caught me by surprise, bursting out of her, air from a ruptured balloon. 'It's not so! It's not so!' She cried, tears flowing fiercely, and then for a long time.

When she stopped and looked up again, I spread my hands to offer myself for convincing. I said, 'I've spelled out what I think and why. Maybe I don't have it all right. Please, sort out the details for me.'

'No,' she said harshly. 'I am not going to talk to you.'

'In that case,' I said, 'I feel I have no alternative but to go to the police.'

She reacted facially to the word, but again grew silent.

I said, 'Maybe you should think over what I've said.'

Snappishly, 'Yes, yes. I will think it over.'

'And,' I said, 'discuss it with . . . your friends.'

To agree to this would have conceded something. She did not speak.

'Just don't take long about it,' I said. I got up and left the house.

TWENTY-FOUR

I drove out of the Belters', but headed away from the city at the end of the drive. Up the road I turned around and pulled over to wait.

My engine hardly had time to catch its breath when a small Japanese car pulled out of the Belters' driveway and headed for Indianapolis. I couldn't see clearly, but I was certain that it was being driven by a small Japanese woman.

I also was reasonably sure that I knew where the car was leading me.

We passed taxi stands and bus stops as we got closer to the centre of the city. They put me in mind of Bates' description of tailing Vera Edwards, that she knew enough to change her means of transport to try to shake anyone who might be following. It struck me as a funny thing for a country girl to be knowledgeable enough to do. But a country girl who has learned to sing for her living gets to know a lot of funny things.

Tamae Mitsuki drove straight as an arrow to Tarkington Tower. She walked into the lobby hurriedly. I drew up outside the front doors to watch. She didn't look back. She pushed a bell on the intercom unit, but then opened the locked door with a key.

I wondered if she would be expressionless with Normal

201

Bates when he asked her whether I had followed her and she had to confess that she didn't think to look.

I considered parking and joining them but decided not to. It was their time to adjust to the fact that their secrets were shared.

Instead I went to police headquarters.

Just inside the main entrance I ran into Leroy Powder.

He said, 'Decided to give yourself up?'

'I've come to see Miller.'

'Got some more errands for him, gumshoe?'

'I'm making progress. You want to hear about it?'

'Have you found the rich lady that knocked off her old man yet?'

'No.'

'Then I'll pass.'

I expected him to leave. But he didn't. He said, 'I had a trainee civilian in yesterday. Young kid. Stupid, but we got such a workload you got to try to use anything they send to you these days.'

'Yeah?' I said.

'Supposed to know his way around computer information systems so I thought up a few make-work jobs for him.'

'Yeah?'

'I tried him on that houseboy, Mitsuki. See if he could get anything from California. Now, Christ, something like that ought to be easy enough, even for a trainee. Wouldn't you think that, Samson? Wouldn't you think that?'

'Yeah, yeah,' I said. 'So, did he come up with anything?'

'I nearly had to do the whole thing for him myself. He's that bad.'

'Did you find anything out?'

'Oh. You in a hurry? Why didn't you say so? We tracked down a Koichi Mitsuki that died of pneumonia in '42 in a camp for Japanese called Manzano. We get the right one?'

'Yeah,' I said.

'So there the trail ends for the missing houseboy. Unless you can track his wife and kid. You know he had a wife and kid?'

I nodded.

'Name of wife Tamae Seto? Married September 20th, 1940?'

'I didn't have her maiden name,' I said.

'Kid named Hiroshi. That's a boy. Only child.'

'Yes,' I said.

'Jesus, no flies on you, gumshoe,' he said. 'Born November 13th, 1940.'

I raised my eyebrows.

'I finally got to something interesting, huh?' he said, smiling. 'Didn't know she had a kid who was seven months premature?'

'No.'

'Well,' he said, 'the Japanese never suffered from the same kind of Victorianism we did, so I read. Bit of a mover this Koichi Mitsuki?'

'The kid wasn't his,' I said sombrely. Suddenly I felt a wall of my edifice of speculation crumbling. Maybe Koichi Mitsuki had needed no money to be offered the opportunity to marry quickly into Tamae's family. The willingness to take on another man's child might have given him the shortcut. And maybe also given Tamae Mitsuki reason to leave California after the war when she was alone, with a child and a history. Maybe her gratitude to Koichi *was* enough to make her want to go to the last place he was associated with. Maybe he had told her that Ella Murchison had been a friend to Vera Edwards and so might be to her.

Powder said, 'Your eyes are glazed. Have you just had a stroke?'

'My jigsaw pieces fit together in different ways and I don't know which to choose.'

203

He laughed at me and shook his head slowly. 'Poor gumshoe.'

I said, 'Your trainee ought to have a chance to track someone in California all by himself, now you've shown him how to do it. He'll never learn otherwise.'

Powder said, 'What did you have in mind?'

'Check for Vera Edwards.'

'The rich lady,' he said, starchily. 'I remember.' He glared.

'It's a reasonable place for a woman with money to lose herself. She was pregnant too. Your trainee could look for a birth somewhere, August through December 1940, to a mother named Vera or Daisy, Wert, Edwards or Wines.'

'Any special reason to suspect California?'

'I think she contacted Koichi Mitsuki.'

'Contacted,' he repeated.

'Yeah.'

'As in it could have been a telephone call?'

It could have been. I nodded.

'Go waste somebody else's time,' Powder said.

I went upstairs to Miller's office.

He wasn't there and they didn't know when he would be back.

Having enjoyed a certain heady feeling of accomplishment earlier in the day, I was dropping like a diver off the high board who was wondering whether there was really water in the pool down there after all.

A new slant wasn't necessarily more right than an old one. But I was subject to the disquiet of wanting to know answers to things I didn't even have the right questions for.

Before I left the police department I wrote a note asking Miller to call me, and I tried to talk to the duty detective about whether there had been any information from the reconstruction at the Biarritz.

But there had been no progress.

I went home. The snow was beginning to stick on the sidewalks.

TWENTY-FIVE

I was having a late lunch of pickle and peanut butter sandwiches when somebody entered my outer office.

I wasn't in the mood, so I didn't bound up, dash to the door, bow, scrape.

Still, pickle doesn't go that well with peanut butter.

I found that my visitor was none other than Roger the Agency Op, last seen about to visit Normal Bates for Wanda Edwards.

'Roger!' I said.

He was surveying my reception chamber. A wisp of a smile showed as he turned to me. 'Mr Samson?'

'My friends call me "sir," but don't feel obliged. Sit down. If you're staying.'

He looked around the room. I have a bench and a chair for clients. He didn't look taken with either but he finally chose the chair.

'How'd you get on with Norm?'

'How did you know who I was?' he asked.

'I recognised you from Jane's description. Great way with words, Jane.'

He rubbed the back of his head. I felt he was getting annoyed. But he forced himself into a working gear. He said, 'Miss Wanda Edwards hired me through my agency a couple of days ago to locate her sister-in-law.'

'I know,' I said.

He nodded as if it had been front-page news and everybody should know. 'But I don't know why the hell my controller took the case on. We're rushed off our feet. Seems everybody in the whole damn city wants something investigated. You probably have the same problem.'

'My feet hardly remember what the floor is like,' I said.

'I don't usually work on weekends,' he said.

'Me neither.'

'But when the clients are ready to pay for speed, it's hard to turn them down.'

'I couldn't agree more.'

'So,' he said, 'once I found out that there was another operative working on the same case, but for different people, I thought to myself, what are we both killing ourselves for? We're pros. If the trail is there, we'll both find it. So, I thought, why not stop by and talk to the other guy, man to man. If we pool our resources, and work together, then we find the lady more quickly and with less fuss.'

'Normal Bates got fussed, huh?'

'Frankly, for someone who knows what the job is about, he didn't cooperate a lot. I couldn't seem to find a way to get to him.'

'Oh dear,' I said.

'I don't know what terms you are on with your client – Douglas Belter, the banker, isn't it? But, to be honest and frank with you, my client has come in with a money-is-no-object attitude, and there would be no problem in doubling up a substantial part of your fee. Especially if we can crack it quickly. I'm going to be straight with you. I think you're probably a little ahead of me just at the moment. But you know how useful the kind of facilities I have access to through the agency could be. Thing is, I've got an industrial case that I am due to start on Monday, a big undercover thing, and if there's any way I can clear this one by then, well, I've got to go for it. So. . . .'

He paused.

Maybe deciding whether to call me Mr Samson or sir.

'What facilities have you got?'

'Everything to make modern detection easier. Direct computer links to almost every information bank in Indiana and most of the major storage facilities nationwide. Supplemental agents. Contacts in the Police Department, State Police, Sheriff's Office and Midwest FBI, as well as a number of governmental and private service agencies like IRS and banks. All kinds of live and remote surveillance equipment. And anything we don't have we can get.'

'That's impressive,' I said.

'It's a hell of an outfit,' he said. 'Everything first class.'

'So let me get the situation clear, Roger,' I said. 'You are completely stuck and want to get off the hook by buying me out. Do I take the gist of things correctly?'

He was not struck by my evaluation.

'I like you a lot, Rog, old pal. You got real style. But I'm one of these old-fashioned girls. The kind that might give it away, but doesn't like being asked to sell it.'

The agency-trained smile gave way to a purely private glare.

He said, 'You're saying fuck off?'

'Right.'

He stood and seemed to swell to an awesome size in front of me.

'I ought to know better than to try to deal in a professional manner with an amateur penny-ante creep. You guys are scavengers, jackals who feed on the remains that big-time outfits leave behind. You live off the sick business we wouldn't touch, or on the muscle game, and the kind of image we do everything possible to put behind us. If I didn't despise guys like you, working alone or in tiddly shit agencies, I'd feel sorry for you.'

208

He backed to the door, and left. He didn't say goodbye.

My pal Rog cheered me up a lot because, whatever else he may be, a jackal disinclined to sell his clients out has got to be a jackal of distinction.

TWENTY-SIX

Just before three I got two phone calls from Police Headquarters.

The first was from Leroy Powder.

When I answered my phone he said, 'Go away. I want to talk to your machine.'

'Pretend,' I said.

'The message is that there is no record of a birth in California, August to December 1940, to a woman with any of the combinations of name you gave me.'

'Oh,' I said.

He hung up.

Miller was the second caller.

'I have a message that I should get in touch.'

'I'm looking for a favour. You can hardly refuse the man who introduced you to Wendy Winslow.'

'One day maybe,' he said. 'But not today.'

'It ought to be simple enough. I need a taxable income history.'

'IRS?' he asked. 'That's supposed to be easy?'

'All the private eye agencies can get them. I've just had a guy in here saying so.'

'I'm not saying it can't be done.' He sounded thoughtful.

'The taxpayer is one Tamae Mitsuki.'

I spelled it for him.

'And I'm looking for 1946 onwards.'

210

'How soon?'

'Ten minutes?'

He laughed.

'There is a possible tie-up with the Murchison case.'

'Ah,' he said. 'The housekeeper.'

'That's right.'

I heard the furrow on his brow manifest itself. 'What's happening, Al?'

'If her income is bigger than it ought to be, then it supports an involvement.'

'She was the last person associated with the family to see Murchison alive,' he said.

'I'm not saying she did it.' Then, for a moment, I wondered if I was.

'An involvement,' Miller said, stressing each syllable of the words I'd used.

'According to one of my scenarios.'

'How does it go?'

'I'm still in rehearsals.'

'I would like to know, Al.'

'And somebody's just come into the office.'

'Like hell.'

Suddenly, I heard somebody come into the office.

'I wouldn't lie to you, Jerry.'

I went.

My visitor was Glass Albert Connah, landlord. He looked unseasonably gloomy.

'Cheer up,' I said. 'If one of Santa's reindeer breaks down on the way to your house, he's bound to have a spare roped to the back of the sleigh.'

'Feel like shooting some hoops?' he asked.

The weather was poor, and he didn't have sneakers on.

'Sure,' I said.

We went outside to the backboard and basket mounted

at the back of the residential section of the property. The light was fading and there was slush in the key. I gave him the ball and cleared a little space with a snow shovel. He bounces the ball each time before he shoots. It's a technical point, a fault. I'm great on coaching tips.

We played 'long and short', in coats and gloves.

In the middle of the second game I asked, 'What's the problem?'

'Glass,' he said.

'Doesn't the insurance cover it?'

'Oh yes. But it doesn't seem sensible to restock when the cash might be better used on other things.'

He shot for a while, but blew the turn on an easy short.

As he handed the ball to me he said, 'And I've had an offer for the place.'

During his next turn I tried to remember the terms of the agreement we had drawn up when I moved in. Which was due to cover ten years. And which represented more security of office tenure than I had ever had before.

'You going to take it?' I said.

'I'm thinking about it,' he said, and the ball zinged hard off the back of the rim so that by the time he caught up with it, his short was considerably longer than his long.

'I see.'

He made the shot.

'We'll come to an agreement.'

'Have you already decided?'

'Not yet.'

My hands were cold from the wet of the ball penetrating the gloves. He won the game and left.

I took a shower and luxuriated in the warmth of the water. It made me feel physically good and I cheered up. I remembered that in 1953 two songs were released almost the same day: 'Santa Got Stuck in the Chimney' and 'When Santa Got Stuck in the Chimney'. Only one of them became a hit, which was poor return for the other guy with the same idea.

It showed there is no justice in life.

I was being evicted for Christmas.

But what can you do?

TWENTY-SEVEN

I cleaned house for about an hour.

I stopped to telephone the Belters. Nobody answered.

I found myself worrying. When one person in a family has been murdered unexpectedly it shakes confidence in your ability to predict happenings.

I wondered what to do. I did nothing.

At about five Normal Bates called.

'Can you come here, now?' he asked.

'I've just been cleaning and polishing the place so I wouldn't be ashamed to have visitors.'

'I would prefer you to come here,' he said. He sounded sad.

The door to the apartment was ajar and when I entered, Bates and Tamae Mitsuki sat facing me, looking a strained and tired pair.

From somewhere a third chair had been produced, because the one I was now accustomed to using was still in its place in front of the computer equipment.

'Take a seat,' Bates said.

I pulled the chair out, placed it to face them and sat. I said, 'I want nothing but the truth this time. If I scent anything else I'll be out of here like a shot. And that's not what you want, is it?'

'No,' Bates said. 'It's not.'

I addressed Tamae Mitsuki. 'Where is Vera Edwards?'

'She lives in New York.'

'Where in New York? What's the address?'

'Mr Samson, she does not want us to tell you.'

'Why not?'

'The more general question,' Normal Bates interjected, 'is why she doesn't want to make herself known to her daughter.'

'Agreed.'

'The bottom line is that she does not have the emotional strength to get directly involved with Mrs Belter,' Bates said.

'She's not well,' Tamae Mitsuki added.

I tensed. 'You better spell it out.'

Tamae Mitsuki said, 'Mrs Edwards remarried. She had three children. Six years ago her husband died of cancer and her mental health was affected. She was not completely stable before that, but since her husband died she has had two periods of hospitalisation. A husband dying is a terrible thing.'

I sat.

Bates said, 'She retains an interest in Mrs Belter. She always felt guilty that she left her behind in Indianapolis. But she is adamant that she doesn't want direct contact to be made. She says that her medical advisers support that position completely.'

'So you can put me in contact with these medical advisers?'

They looked at each other. 'If absolutely necessary,' Bates said.

'And you two are both on her payroll?'

'Yes,' Bates said.

'You keep her up to date with family affairs and get back to her for instructions when special situations come up?'

215

'You are the only special situation that ever came up,' Tamae Mitsuki said.

'It's not me. It's the phony birth certificate that started this. You were responsible for that?'

'Yes,' Bates said. 'It was needed when Paula got married.'

'In order not to spoil her happiness,' Tamae Mitsuki said.

A sarcastic edge came into my voice as I asked, 'And you've both just been following orders?'

'Not . . .' Tamae Mitsuki began.

Bates said, 'We have acted on our own initiative since the "situation" arose. Though Mrs Edwards has subsequently approved our actions.'

'Actions,' I repeated. 'Like hiring me to keep an eye on me?'

'Yes,' Bates said.

'And trying to buy me off with your must-start-immediately six-month job?'

'Yes.'

'And shooting my landlord's glass up, and offering to buy out the property I live in?'

Tamae Mitsuki turned to Bates and said, 'Normal, you didn't say anything about—'

Bates interrupted her. 'I know nothing about either of those things.'

'And which one of you killed Ella Murchison?'

'Not that,' Tamae Mitsuki said forcefully.

'Well, how was it done? Did Mrs Edwards come back specially from New York to do it herself?'

Tamae Mitsuki burst into tears.

Normal Bates looked grave. 'Mrs Edwards was as shocked and surprised as any of us when that happened, Mr Samson. And we are certainly as eager to identify Mrs Murchison's killer as you are.'

'We loved her!' Tamae Mitsuki said, and the act of speaking helped to calm her.

'Who gained advantage from her death besides Mrs Edwards?' I asked.

'I don't know,' Bates said.

'Mrs Edwards didn't get any advantage from her dying,' Tamae Mitsuki said.

'Of course she did,' I snapped. 'It guaranteed Mrs Murchison wouldn't tell anybody the truth.'

'She would never have told the truth.'

We weren't getting anywhere. So I tacked. 'Where did Mrs Edwards go after the trial?'

'To New York,' Bates said.

'And how—'

'Before she left Indianapolis, she arranged to keep in touch with Koichi Mitsuki because she realised he would be fired by the Edwards family for testifying in her support.'

'And she helped him financially?'

I looked at Tamae Mitsuki. 'She offered, but he refused,' she said. 'But after he died I agreed to come back to Indianapolis for her.'

'For which she paid you?'

'Yes.'

'And set your son up in his restaurant?'

'She . . . helped.'

'So the financial contribution has been considerable.'

'Yes,' she said, unapologetically.

'And how much did you get, Mr Bates?'

'An annual retainer,' he said.

'I mean to perjure yourself at the trial.'

The bright eyes burned. 'Absolutely nothing. What I told you before about that was true.'

'But you did help her with arrangements to leave Indianapolis?'

217

'Yes.'

'And you did conspire with her to arrange circumstances so that she could kill her husband, inherit a fortune, and get away with it.'

'I conspired nothing. Absolutely nothing,' he said furiously. I began to be glad he was old and that I could surely defend myself. 'I did what was right. What I thought was right and what I still think was right. I believed then and I believe now that she was innocent of murder.'

'I too am certain she didn't murder him,' Tamae Mitsuki added gratuitously. 'Sometimes things can look bad but still not be.'

'Well,' I said, 'why don't you call up Mrs Edwards now and let me ask her myself.'

'She doesn't want to be called again today,' Tamae Mitsuki said. 'By any of us.'

'In that case I'll just push off and go to the police,' I said. I rose and headed for the door.

'We hope you won't feel you have to go to the police or anybody else,' Bates said. I stopped and turned back to him. 'But we are bound by Mrs Edwards' instructions, so go if you must.'

I scowled, and returned to my seat. 'What is she, a female Howard Hughes?'

'She is just unwell,' Tamae Mitsuki said.

'How about I talk to her tomorrow?'

'We could try to arrange it,' she said.

'Or maybe I should just go to New York?'

She said, 'I can ask her. But Mr Samson, I don't understand why you insist on making life unpleasant for poor Mrs Edwards. You've been hired by Mr and Mrs Belter for a much more limited purpose.'

'My current instruction is to find Mrs Belter's mother.'

'But if Mrs Belter's mother doesn't want to be found, for good reasons?'

'Mrs Belter's mother is not my client.'

'And are you not capable of looking at the circumstances and making a moral decision?' Bates asked rhetorically, still angry at the accusations I'd made.

'What would you have me tell my clients, Mrs Mitsuki?'

'If I had my choice?'

'Yeah. Free choice.'

'That Mrs Edwards died long ago.'

'And if they asked about the dispersal of the estate?'

'That Mrs Edwards settled half her resources in trust funds for Mrs Belter's children. The other half went to her other children.'

'Is that what she's done?'

'Yes.'

'But the Belters don't know?'

'No.'

'Shouldn't they be told?'

'Tell them,' she said.

I leaned back in my chair and scratched my head. Then I scratched it again.

'How can I possibly trust you people?'

'Because what we say is true,' Tamae Mitsuki said.

'What's wrong with my telling the Belters that Mrs Edwards is alive but for reasons of health doesn't want to make contact?'

'All right,' Mrs Mitsuki said, 'tell her that. It leaves things open when Paula needs the situation to be finished, but she can adjust to what you suggest, in time. Especially. . . .'

I waited.

'Especially if your scruples will allow you not to tell her that I deceived her. She relies on me for emotional support and it would be a great blow to her. Beyond all things, that is what I wish to convince you to avoid.'

'Beyond all things?' I asked. 'Beyond saying that I think

219

Mrs Edwards is a murderer?'

'She isn't a murderer,' Tamae Mitsuki said.

'But . . . ?'

'But beyond that, yes,' she said.

'What are you going to do, Samson?' Normal Bates asked.

'I don't know,' I said honestly. 'Think. Maybe talk to the Belters and sound them out on some of the alternatives.' I asked Mrs Mitsuki, 'Where are they, by the way? They don't seem to be at home.'

'They've gone to meet the boys. Both are flying in today for the funeral. Their planes are due within forty-five minutes of each other so they are all meeting up at the airport.'

I sat looking from one to the other for a few moments.

'What sours everything is the killing of Ella Murchison,' I said.

Neither of them had anything to add on that subject.

TWENTY-EIGHT

I left Tarkington Tower in a ragged state.

I had wrought admissions. Admissions I had expected to be proud of and which constituted new information for my clients.

But I didn't feel that I had a grip on what was right, what was wrong.

I didn't feel, in my gut, that I knew which way I should go.

It took me the whole drive home to realise that I meant I shouldn't 'go' anywhere. Yet.

The answering machine showed that there had been a telephone call while I was out, but instead of listening to the message I attended to more important telecommunication.

I called my woman. I invited her to come out for a meal.

Then encouraged her, pleaded, begged.

She finally agreed. 'For old times' sake,' she said.

I felt humble. In theory, I value friendship above all things. In practice, I get over-involved in work.

Life is too short. It's people that count and if you have some you can feel for, they should be treated well. I missed my daughter. 'I'm sorry,' I said.

The call was from Miller, who left a message: 'The IRS has

no record of tax returns from a Tamae Mitsuki.'

I found that puzzling. But after entering the statement in my notebook, I flipped the thing closed and left it in a desk drawer.

I picked my woman up a few minutes after seven. I had showered. I had tied. A special occasion.

She took my hand in the doorway. 'I should know what you are like by now,' she said.

Later I offered her food.

'Something different,' she said.

My face showed I was worried.

'There's a place I have never tried,' I said, as if there were only one, 'but it has a connection to the case I may or may not still be working on.'

'That's all right,' she said.

The restaurant was The Rising Sun, owned by Tamae Mitsuki's son. Carefully and generously decorated, it was rather more than a restaurant, boasting regular entertainment at weekends.

The visible employees were all Oriental but the menu was only fifty percent Japanese, the other half drawing on cuisine from several countries. It was a flash place. I had an aperitif and didn't feel self-conscious.

I fell quickly into devoting myself to wine and woman. Singing I don't do so good.

For a while I felt great, positively hirundine as we swooped and soared through reacquaintance.

I only came down to earth when I asked the waiter to send my compliments to the owner.

'Would you like to speak to him yourself?' He turned towards a short, chubby man talking seriously to two diners at a nearby table. His features were only mildly Oriental and a black suit emphasised a pale complexion.

222

'That's Hiroshi Mitsuki?' I asked.

'Yes. The proprietor,' the waiter said. 'I bring him over.'

'No!'

I grounded with a thud.

My woman friend was fully aware of my descent. She apologised for me and then said quietly, 'Tell me about it.'

Gratefully I explained about the two problems I was grappling with: who killed Mrs Murchison and the truth about Vera Edwards.

About Mrs Murchison's murder my woman asked, 'If your dynamic duo wasn't responsible, who could be?'

On the other one I thought I was ahead of her. She asked, 'Do you believe this Edwards woman *is* alive?'

'I do now,' I said. 'And not in New York.'

Talking out problems you are confused about can be a wonderful thing. Fresh perspectives are often as good as fresh information. And when you get both, it is gravy.

When we finished I felt I finally understood what had happened. And what responsibility I bore.

I also had a rough idea how to test part of my theory. If I could manage to obtain a little assistance.

I spent some of the time I should have been sleeping working out details. I slept the rest feeling that I stood a reasonable chance of precipitating some confirmations of what I thought.

You can't be right about everything.

TWENTY-NINE

First thing Saturday morning I called the National Security Service and asked to speak to their agent named Roger. 'I never did get his last name,' I said sweetly.

After a minute of internal inquiry the honeyed voice of the agency receptionist, more honeyed even than mine, told be that Mr Claypool was not on the premises but was expected to call in soon. Would I like to leave a message?

I would. 'Please tell Mr Claypool that Mr Samson has located Mrs Vera Edwards and he would be happy to share the information if suitable terms can be agreed. Mr Samson will be at home all morning.'

I called the Belters' house.

Tamae Mitsuki answered the telephone.

'Could you get Mr Belter for me, please?'

She was silent for several seconds. 'May I ask why?'

'There is a favour I want to ask him, having to do with Mrs Murchison's murder.'

She hesitated again, but I interrupted the silence. 'I'm short of time.'

Douglas Belter came to the telephone.

'Hello, Samson. I'm afraid that I have rather neglected you of late.'

'You sound more cheerful, Mr Belter.'

'It's having the boys home. A sad occasion, of course, but

they do wonders for Paula. And last night Cab told us that he's invited a girl to come out, for the holidays. They plan to be married. Paula is in a terrible flap about it, but she's thrilled.'

'I'm pleased for you.'

'Thank you,' he said. 'But Tamae said something about Ella's murder.' He paused. 'It's a terrible thing to say, but that seems a long time ago already.'

'I don't want to disturb your plans while your children are here,' I said, 'but I would like to borrow your house for a while. . . .'

I called Miller.

The detective desk officer was not honey-voiced. But I was put straight through. I asked him how his Murchison investigation was going.

'It's not,' Miller said.

'The reconstruction didn't help?'

'Not substantively,' he said. He paused for a moment. I could kind of feel him thinking. He said, 'Albert, what is on your mind?'

'Would you be interested in taking a shot at clearing it all up?'

'A "shot"? Meaning what?'

'Meaning creating circumstances which would encourage the killer to self-exposure.'

He was silent at first. But then he asked, 'When?'

'If it works, it should be quick. Today, probably. If it doesn't, you'll still have a way into it by interrogation, search of premises and so on. But this could tie it up in a stroke.'

'What would it take?'

'You'll have to get a team of three or four together right away. If you're interested.'

He *had* to be interested, given what he had told me about his need for a big case, one with PR content.

'I'm interested,' he said.

225

THIRTY

Roger called at a quarter past ten. He said, 'Before you say anything, I want to apologise for having lost my temper yesterday. I said things that I regret.'

'Don't give it another thought.'

'I have a message that you've located Vera Edwards.'

'That's right.'

'Good work. Congratulations.'

'Thank you.'

'How certain are you of the identification?'

'She answers to the name.'

'You've talked to her?'

'I have.'

'That's really very good.'

Even when there's a reason, I find it hard to be civil when I am patronised. But all I said was, 'Thanks.'

'And you would be willing after all to tell me where she is?'

'Thing is,' I said, 'I've found out that I may have to move to new premises soon.'

'That's rough,' he said.

'Also expensive.'

'I see. How expensive?'

I said, 'What do you think your client could stand?'

'I'm sure my client would run to five hundred. In cash.'

'Oh, no,' I said dismissively.

He thought. 'You know, Mr Samson. . . .'

'Please,' I said, 'call me Albert.'

'Thanks Albert. But I was going to say, I hate bargaining.'

'Me too.'

'So what figure do you want?'

'I was thinking how much five thou would smooth my move.'

'Five thousand dollars?' He sounded shocked.

'You are a long way from the lady,' I said. 'And at the rates you agency fellows charge, I thought that was pretty modest.'

He considered. 'I'll try it on her,' he said. 'But tell me what you'll take if she won't go that high.'

'What say we split anything over four five? So you can show something for your trouble,' I said.

'I'll see what I can do. If it's on, when will you give us the information?'

'Just as soon as the cash – shall we say used fifties? – is in my hand.'

'My client would be entitled to confirmation of the identification before any money is transferred.'

'I am an old-fashioned private eye,' I said, 'as you pointed out so forcefully yesterday. One of the characteristics is that my word is my bond.'

He thought about it. There would be ways he could get back at me.

'I'll be in touch,' Roger said.

I sat at home, waiting.

I tried to be constructive. I started to reread my notebook entries.

But sitting was no good. I was reduced to more housecleaning. It was something to do.

Roger Claypool got to my place just after one.

He looked entirely pleased with himself as he and his fancy suit came through my door. 'I have good news, Mr Samson,' he said.

'Super.'

'I got you your four-five.'

I forbore asking how much he got him. He handed me an envelope filled with fifty dollar bills. I counted them. I made it four thousand four hundred and fifty but didn't quibble. I don't get much practice counting that high.

Claypool watched. When I finished he said, 'And now, Vera Edwards' address?'

I gave it to him.

'In Indianapolis all the time?'

'Yes.'

He studied it. 'Fancy part of town.'

'She is a wealthy woman,' I said.

'How did you find her?'

I waved the envelope at him. 'Lessons are extra.'

He rose. Then he pointed a finger at me. 'If there is anything wrong with this information, I wouldn't spend that bread too quickly because sure as shit I'll have it back from you, with interest.'

THIRTY-ONE

I drove out to the Belters' house.

There was a light covering of snow from the previous day's precipitation. It showed a lot of tyre tracks on the drive. But there were no cars. I got out of the van and went to the front door. I rang the bell.

A grey-haired woman's face appeared in the crack as the door was opened.

'Yes?' she said.

'Are you Mrs Edwards?'

'I am.'

'May I come in?'

'All right,' she said.

She stepped back and I entered to find a stocky woman, apparently in her sixties, heavily rouged and powdered.

I had never seen her before. 'You are Vera Wert Edwards?'

'That's right.'

I reached into my jacket pocket for my notebook.

In an instant, both my arms were pulled behind me by what felt like a dozen hands. My limbs were twisted back and up, short only of being tied in a bow.

Then feet kicked repeatedly at my legs. They insisted that I take a dive. Only it was a belly flop, on the hall floor.

I noticed the tiles coming up in time to lift my head away from the first impact. But this haughty distancing didn't last long. A lead beret was fitted from behind, intent on pushing my face into the space already occupied by the floor beneath it. That's against the laws of physics. Something would have to give.

It was almost my nose.

But a disappointed voice interrupted the inevitability of science. It said, 'Back off. Let him up. False alarm.'

I stayed on the floor, panting.

'He isn't dead, is he, Lieutenant?'

I sat up to see a pair of grey dacron legs in front of me. With effort, I lifted my gaze and focused on a brown face. 'You guys play tackle, don't you,' I said.

'You could have said who you were when the door was answered,' Miller said.

'I was interested in what kind of surprise party you and the reception committee had arranged.' I nodded approvingly towards the two detectives who had protected Vera Wert Edwards. They had felt like an army. Behind them the old woman stood waiting with athletic ease.

'She looks good,' I said.

The policewoman took a little bow.

'I'm pleased you're pleased,' Miller said. 'But get up and move your van, will you? I want the driveway clear.' He studied me. 'I can get someone to do it for you.'

'No,' I said, 'I'll do it.'

'All right,' he said. Then, 'I hope this works out.'

'So do I,' I said.

I moved the van to the back of the house and returned to the front door. I called, 'Peace. Friend,' as I went in this time.

Miller took me to the living room.

'Where's the family?' I asked.

'At the funeral service,' Miller said. 'They'll call before they head back here and they'll check with my man out on

230

the road before actually driving in. If it comes to it, I figure the house is plenty big enough for them to stay out of the way for as long as we decide to stick around.'

'And the housekeeper?' I asked.

'I made her stay behind,' Miller said. 'It took some doing but I said I needed someone who knew the house and could cover the phone.'

I nodded. 'Where is she?'

'In the kitchen.'

THIRTY-TWO

Tamae Mitsuki sat on a stool at the breakfast counter nursing a glass of tomato juice. She didn't look up immediately as I came in and she didn't seem surprised to see me when she did.

'Hello,' I said.

'Hello.' The voice seemed flat.

'You sound tired,' I said.

She faced me. 'What's all this about?'

'Didn't they tell you?'

'Only that they are hoping for something that will sort out Ella's murder.'

I took a stool next to her. 'They think that Mrs Murchison's murderer might come here to try to kill Vera Edwards.'

'Vera Edwards?' she asked.

'The idea is that since Vera Edwards is wealthy she would live in a fancy place. So we're using this house.'

She shrugged. She turned to her drink and sipped.

'Besides,' I said, 'since you do live here, Mrs Edwards, it seems only appropriate.'

Tamae Mitsuki was utterly still.

I gave her that long moment of peace. After all, she had been hiding the identity for more than forty years.

But it began to look like she would be silent forever. I couldn't wait that long.

I said, 'I took a friend to Hiroshi's restaurant last night. What made it fall into place was seeing him. That he is clearly not a hundred percent Japanese. It put me to thinking how that could be so.'

She raised her eyes. 'I was raped by a Caucasian sailor.'

'I don't believe you,' I said quietly.

We sat.

'You are no more Japanese than I am,' I said. 'Eye shape and hair, sure, but not the cheek bones, skin colour or eye colour. And your English is as Hoosier as mine. What do we find if we search your room for hair dye? When did you have your eyes operated on, Mrs Edwards? I figure it had to be pretty soon after you left Indianapolis if you were married as "Tamae Seto" by the end of September.'

She looked defiant and stayed silent.

'Since there are surgeons who can "westernise" eye shape for Orientals, a rich woman has to be able to find a surgeon to "Orientalise" her eyes if she wants one. As a gesture to an Oriental husband? To help lose a former self by becoming submerged in a new culture? Or just a pragmatic step to avoid the prejudice against a white woman with a yellow baby? That would have been worse in California then even than in Indianapolis, what with their history of "yellow peril" paranoia. Nothing to say, Mrs Edwards?'

'My name is Mitsuki,' she said. But it was a correction of detail rather than a contradiction of substance.

'All right. Vera Mitsuki.'

'Tamae,' she insisted.

'You had it legally changed?'

Her eyes remained on her glass. She spoke quietly. But she spoke. 'Tamae was Koichi's mother's name. It's a refined, old-fashioned name. Like Lily in English.'

I put my face little more than a foot from hers. 'I have decisions to make before your daughter and her family get

233

back.'

Resignedly she said, 'You will do what you have to.'

'Damn it, I want some answers. Unless you no longer know what is truth and what is fiction.'

Hoosier determination for survival comfortably swamped the learned submissiveness. '*I* know what's happened in my life,' she snapped. 'Nobody else does.'

'That's part of my problem,' I said.

She glared at me.

I glared back. What I decided to do would affect the lives of several people. I didn't just need new answers. I needed some reason to believe them.

'What prompted you to take the houseboy to bed when you were Benny Edwards' wife? Uncontrollable lust?'

She drew a quick breath. 'Benny was vicious and Koichi was the first man who was ever nice to me.'

'If Edwards was vicious, why did you marry him?'

'I didn't know what he was like until after I lived with him. I knew he wasn't nice, but he said he loved me, and I thought that meant something. I thought it would mean I could do well by Paula.'

'If you were sleeping with Koichi, why take Normal Bates to bed?'

'He was . . . so sad. And he wanted to help.'

'Did you screw every man who was nice to you?'

'They are the only two who ever were,' she said.

It was a cold comment on a long life.

'So when you got pregnant, you arranged for your two lovers to help you kill your psychotic husband?'

She said emphatically, 'Nothing was arranged or planned or intended. That night I told Benny that I was going to leave him, since the baby wasn't his. He went crazy. He attacked me. I shot him. It was self-defence. Neither Normal nor Koichi was involved. It just happened.'

'Why didn't you say so at the trial?'

'Normal said it would look bad.'

'It does,' I said.

'I can't help that!' she said explosively. 'True things don't always look true.'

'So you all three lied at the trial.'

'One way or another, yes.'

'And you ran off with the father of your impending child, having shot your husband and become a very rich woman.'

'Koichi and I didn't leave together. But I loved him and we planned to meet.'

'Just as you planned the murder of your husband?'

'There was no plan.'

'Not even in the back of your mind?'

'I hardly had a mind,' she said.

It was almost a concession.

She said, 'I lived with a man who put me in constant physical fear. With his family who hated me. My only relief was to visit my daughter. I tried, Mr Samson. I tried to cope with it all for Paula's sake. It was a terrible responsibility. Unending pressure.' She seemed to relive it.

'Yet you left Paula behind,' I said.

'She was happy where she was. In the circumstances it seemed best for her.' She played with her glass. 'But if I could roll back the years, choose again, I would take her with me.'

'Who is Paula's father?' I asked. 'The Wingfield boy?'

She reacted to the name, surprised that I knew it. 'Yes,' she said.

'Not Michael Carson?'

'Mike? No. Not him.'

'He was nice to you, wasn't he?'

'Not like that. Businesslike.'

'You didn't bed him?'

'I didn't go with anybody else until Koichi.'

'Not with your husband?'

'Not in ways to make babies,' she said.

I was not nearly finished. But we were interrupted by the shots.

THIRTY-THREE

They were muffled, because they came from elsewhere in the house. But I knew the sound immediately.

I ran to the entrance hall.

Miller crouched over the crumpled figure of the athletic policewoman. Her grey wig lay like an aged tarantula in the middle of the floor. There was blood. The front door was open.

'How is she?' I asked.

Miller turned and looked up. 'I don't know.'

'Have you called an ambulance?'

'Of course I've called for an ambulance!' he roared.

I headed for the open door.

I nearly ran into one of the detectives, who was coming into the house.

I stopped and made way for him.

'We got her, Lieutenant. But I think we broke her arm.'

'Go break the other one,' Miller said.

The policewoman groaned.

'Is she all right?'

'I don't know!' Miller said with frustration. He shook his head. 'You give them protective vests and then the lunatic goes for head shots.' He turned to the detective. 'She took one in the side of the head, but I think it's a graze. There's blood on the shoulder and I don't know if there's anything lower down. How many shots did you hear?'

'Two? Three?'

'Three, I think,' Miller said. He looked around. 'Could somebody get me a damp cloth?'

'I will,' Vera Edwards said. She had followed me.

I went outside.

Against the front wall of the house another woman sat. Despite a fur coat and a fur hat she looked tiny beside the policeman who stood above her with his gun pointed at her head. A second, much smaller, gun lay on the driveway, a skid mark in the snow now leading to it.

The policeman was breathing heavily and looked furious.

Wanda Edwards cradled her left arm.

I crouched beside her.

She looked at me without recognition. Only vengeance showed in her eyes. 'Is she dead?' she asked. 'Did I get her this time?'

'Who?' I asked.

'That slut in there, of course. She murdered my brother, you know. It's only justice.'

'Was it justice to kill Ella Murchison?' I asked.

Her concentration seemed to fade as she absorbed my question. 'Kill who?' she asked.

'You killed Ella Murchison,' I said. 'Vera Edwards' friend.'

'That was Ella Murchison? She said she was Vera Edwards. I asked and she said she was Vera Edwards.'

'I don't mean here. You killed Ella Murchison at the Biarritz nursing home.'

'Don't be silly,' she snapped. 'You think I go around shooting everybody in town? I've waited half a life-time for my brother's murderer. But I haven't killed anybody else.'

THIRTY-FOUR

When I told Miller I was leaving he seemed surprised, but he was too busy making the wounded policewoman comfortable to give it much thought.

When he got around to questioning Wanda Edwards he would find for himself that the theory on which we had based the whole exercise was wrong.

I had assumed that the fierce hatred for Vera Edwards had carried over to people associated with Vera Edwards. I had told Wanda Edwards where she could find Ella Murchison. Jane Smith had said Wanda Edwards had gone out, had become active. I had felt responsible.

But I was wrong.

I drove to Tarkington Tower. I buzzed Normal Bates and told him over the intercom that I wanted to tell him what had happened at the Belters' house.

'Is she all right?' he asked.

'Just let me in,' I said. And he did.

The door was ajar. When I entered the living room the silhouette of Bates and his chair appeared as only a minor break in the spectacular view over the city. The early sunset decorated the western side of the sky. It was a glorious sight.

Once again I moved the straight-backed chair from the

computer table and sat facing him.

He didn't face me. He just repeated, slowly and emphatically, 'Is she all right?'

'Yes,' I said. 'Vera Edwards is all right.'

'I knew you knew,' he said, 'when she phoned me to say that she had been asked to stay behind even though it meant missing Ella's funeral.' He was silent for a few seconds. Then he said, 'I will never forgive you for making her miss it.'

'Will she ever forgive you for killing Ella Murchison?'

There was a silence before he said, 'No. Not if she finds out.'

'Just how do you expect her not to find out?'

He turned his chair to face mine, and although the light in the room was not very strong, it was plenty good enough for me to make out a large pearl-handled revolver on his lap.

'Oh, I see!' I said. 'You blow me away. And then you knock off the people who saw you at the Biarritz. And then—'

'People saw me, but nobody noticed,' he said. 'I dressed down and who notices an old man in an old people's home?'

'Someone might have,' I said. 'Have you got enough shells for that thing to cover all contingencies? Have you got enough for my cop friend, who will work it out eventually? And for all his cop friends once you blow him away? No, no, no, Mr Bates. You know as well as I do that there just isn't any point.'

He said nothing.

'Besides,' I said, 'I think she already suspects.'

'It's not the same as knowing,' he said.

We considered that for a moment.

'Why *did* you kill Ella?'

His hands gripped each other. He said, 'I never saw her after 1940, you know. And recently all I'd heard about was

240

this fixation with poisons. I knew Vera was worried because of the pressure Paula was putting on. So I tried to balance what sort of life Ella had left against the damage she might do to Vera. Ella didn't have anything to look forward to. And Vera is a young woman yet. The more I thought about it, the more it seemed the only way to put the lid back on, where it belonged. I have a friend who let me have the doings. Ella was asleep when I got there and it seemed that if I used the drug there was a good chance they would think she just died. It was a reasonable risk at the time.'

I thought of my meeting with Ella Murchison. That she had had more than enough wits about her to keep me at bay. That she had friends, and pleasures.

'You murdered her in cold blood.'

'I shortened her life a little bit,' Bates said. 'That's the worst you can say. I speeded up the inevitable.'

'Oh, great,' I said. 'And you sounded so convincing yesterday when you were lecturing me about moral decisions. You almost had me believing I was a heel for quibbling at perjury to get your mistress off a murder charge.'

'If it means anything to you, I regret what I've done,' Bates said quietly.

I thought about it. 'I suppose that's worth something.'

He glanced away from me, then stared into my eyes. 'Mr Samson, is there anything, anything at all, that I can do, give or say that would keep you from telling Vera what I have done?'

I looked at his bright eyes. Then I looked away.

'Think what I am offering. Think how much the quality of your life could be improved. Right or wrong, what's happened cannot be undone.'

'Your argument for expediency doesn't have the same compelling ring to it that the one for morality had.'

241

He sniffed. 'Your romanticism is almost a certifiable disease.'

We were both silent for a minute. Then I said, 'I think it's time for me to go.'

I rose, and put the chair back in its place before the computer.

As I walked to the door I heard the revolver's hammer click behind me. But I didn't feel afraid and I didn't turn around.

He waited till the door was closed and locked behind me before he did the only thing that might keep me quiet.

THIRTY-FIVE

I made an anonymous telephone call to the police. I had been walking past apartment 1203 when. . . .

Then I dialled the Belters' number. Vera Edwards answered. I asked her whether Miller was still there. She said that he had left with his prisoner a few minutes after the ambulance had collected the policewoman.

'How is she?'

'They say it's not serious,' Vera Edwards said.

I was very much relieved.

'What did Lieutenant Miller say about Wanda Edwards?'

'That he thought she had killed Ella.'

'I see.'

'Did she kill Ella?' Vera Edwards asked.

'Let me talk to Mr Belter, will you?'

She hesitated, but in the gap I heard voices in the background.

The receiver was transferred and Paula Belter burst into my ear. 'Tamae says that is Mr Samson. Is it Mr Samson?'

'Hello Mrs Belter.'

'Have you heard the good news?'

'Which good news is that?'

'I'm going to be a mother-in-law! I've been practising being wicked, but the picture Chip's shown me is so beautiful I just don't think I'm going to be able to rise to the part. She's wonderful and they want to get married in June and I just *love* her!'

'I'm pleased for you,' I said, but while I did so I was being transferred again.

Douglas Belter's voice said, 'Tamae said you want a word with me, Samson. If I can get a little space here. Thank you.'

Even Belter's grey personality came across more silver, a reflection of his wife's ecstasies.

I said, 'I would like to talk to you. Preferably alone.'

He said, 'Well, if it's necessary, I suppose I could come in for a chat.'

'This evening?'

'All right. Is it by way of a wrap-up?'

'Probably.'

'Although I haven't given it much thought, I think it's fair to say we don't feel the urgency about things that we did before.'

'Give it to me, Doug,' Paula Belter said near him. She took the telephone and bubbled to me, 'We couldn't go to Europe this summer now even if we still wanted to, what with the wedding. Isn't it a wonderful anniversary present, Mr Samson? What could be better?'

I left the phone booth and went home to a depressed solitude.

I didn't make any notes.

I didn't do any thinking.

I put some effort into cooking myself a palatable meal and sat down with it in front of the television in time to watch the local news on WTRH.

The wounded policewoman was the lead item. The reporter was Tanya Wilkerson and she interviewed Miller live.

Tanya!

Miller came across well, projecting the solidity and competence we like to associate with our law enforcement personnel. He praised highly the bravery of the officer whom I had put into the line of fire.

But I was able to deduce that he had had time to talk to Wanda Edwards: while he explained that Miss Edwards would be charged with attempted murder and that the situation which had led to the arrest had arisen from information supplied to him by a personal source, he said nothing about the Murchison murder.

And he wouldn't need to. I would tell him what I knew and he could close the case quietly.

There would still be plenty of PR for him as he gradually revealed more background to the press. Tanya would love it when she found out that Wanda Edwards had already tried to kill Vera Edwards, forty odd years before.

I finished my meal and washed up the dishes.

THIRTY-SIX

Douglas Belter was the first of two visitors that evening. He came in just before eight. We went to my inner office.

I asked, 'Is your wife still flying high on the wedding and plans?'

Sombrely he said, 'She's magnificent when she's like this. So full of life.'

We waited to see who was going to start saying the serious things.

It had to be me. I said, 'The woman Lieutenant Miller arrested was looking for Vera Edwards.'

He examined me. 'What reason did this woman have for believing that Vera Edwards was at my house?' He stopped. 'Vera Edwards is alive, isn't she?'

'Yes,' I said.

'And nearby?'

'Yes,' I said.

'Oh.'

'The last day or so you've not been available for me to talk to.'

He looked at me directly and asked, 'Is the news about her bad?'

I said, 'It is complicated.'

We were both quiet for a moment, but before he asked anything else I said, 'I have decided that you should have a talk with Mrs Mitsuki. Tell her I think she should be frank with you.'

'With . . . Tamae,' he stated. Then, 'Oh,' and I felt he suddenly understood. Though he looked disbelieving.

I said, 'Perhaps you can sort out what to say between you. And when. She has opinions on what would be best, but you'll make up your own mind.'

He nodded, very slowly.

'Your wife will ask questions again, before long,' I said.

'Of course,' he said. 'Yes.' Then he asked, 'And this woman they arrested today?'

I said, 'Vera Edwards' husband's sister.'

'I see. And did she kill Ella?'

'I think Lieutenant Miller is still uncertain who killed Mrs Murchison.'

'But . . . not . . . ?'

'No. Definitely not Mrs Edwards.'

Belter said slowly, 'May I have a beer, Mr Samson?'

I got it for him with pleasure.

Before he left I also gave him the photograph of Vera Wert and her family which I had bought in Peru from her sister.

When I was alone again, I called my lady friend. She agreed to come out for a drink.

As I got off the phone my second visitor arrived. Albert Connah, landlord.

He asked for beer too. I told him I was about to leave.

'I'll drink it fast,' he said.

I got him a can and we sat.

By way of conversation he said, 'My son is an asshole.'

'Oh?'

'He's decided he wants to become a community worker, maybe get into politics.'

'Oh.'

'I used to hope the kid would go to law school and come

247

into the business. I'm glad he didn't now. Who could take advice from a kid that ends up wanting to go into politics?'

I watched him for a moment. I said, 'You've decided to sell this place, haven't you?'

'What? Oh. Yeah. Too good a deal to turn down. But that's not what I wanted to tell you. I think maybe I have somewhere else, might even be better for you.'

I didn't say anything for several seconds. Then I said, 'You arranged for those two men to come here and shoot up your glass, didn't you?'

We looked at each other for a long moment.

I said, 'I can't take another place from you.'

He drained the beer and stood up. 'If you change your mind, let me know,' he said. He went to the door, but before he left he said, 'Price of glass just wasn't going up as fast as I expected. Then this offer came along . . .' He shrugged. 'It's a hard world out there, Al.' He left.

Although I was late, I tidied a few things up before I set off.

The first was the $4500 in used fifties Wanda Edwards had paid me for fingering Vera Edwards. Originally I thought to give it to Miller. And then I thought, no. Rather than rush I would think about giving it to something worthy – the helping hand programme that had the sticker in Miller's window maybe. It felt the only way I would be able to say to myself that one small, good thing had come out of all the ugliness of the case.

Then I locked away my notebook. It crossed my mind that bestseller-writer Jane Smith might eventually seek me out one day. She had said that Wanda Edwards told her 'a weird story about her brother's murder.' If Jane Smith had anything about her she would follow it all up, one day. Perhaps I would help her.

And, finally, I got out Charlie Carson's photograph.

*

My lady friend and I went to Carson's Rovers Lounge. We had a terrific time returning the huge man's picture and drinking in his grin when he saw that it hadn't been damaged. We drank other things too, and watched the floor show, and ate, and didn't talk at all about the future, beyond the night to come.

NO EXIT PRESS

There is an extensive list of NO EXIT PRESS crime titles to choose from. All the books can be obtained from Oldcastle Books Ltd, 18 Coleswood Road, Harpenden, Herts AL5 1EQ by sending a cheque/P.O. (or quoting your credit card number and expiry date) for the appropriate amount + 10% as a contribution to Postage & Packing.

Alternatively, you can send for FREE details of the NO EXIT PRESS CRIME BOOK CLUB, which includes many special offers on NO EXIT PRESS titles and full information on forthcoming books. Please write clearly stating your full name and address.

NO EXIT PRESS Vintage Crime

Classic crime novels by the contemporaries of Chandler & Hammett that typify the hard-boiled heyday of American crime fiction.

FAST ONE — Paul Cain £3.95pb, £9.95hb

Possibly the toughest, tough-guy story ever written. Set in depression Los Angeles, it has a surreal quality that is positively hypnotic. It is the saga of gunman-gambler Gerry Kells and his dipsomaniacal lover, S Granquist (she has no first name), who rearrange the L.A. underworld and disappear in an explosive climax that matches their first appearance. The pace is incredible and the complex plot, with its twists and turns, defies summary.

SEVEN SLAYERS — Paul Cain £3.99pb, £9.95hb

A superb collection of seven stories about seven star crossed killers and the sole follow up to the very successful Fast One. Peopled by racketeers, con men, dope pushers, private detectives, cops, newspapermen and women of some virtue or none at all. Seven Slayers is as intense a 'noir' portrait of depression era America as those painted by Horace McCoy and James M Cain.

THE DEAD DON'T CARE — Jonathan Latimer £3.95pb, £9.95hb

Meet Bill Crane, the hard-boiled P.I., and his two sidekicks, O'Malley and Doc Williams. The locale of the cyclonic action is a large Florida estate near Miami. A varied cast includes a former tragic actress turned dipso, a gigolo, a 'Babe' from Minsky's, a broken down welterweight and an exotic Mayan dancer. Kidnapping and murder give the final shake to the cocktail and provide an explosive and shocking climax.

ACT OF FEAR — Michael Collins £2.99 (available 6/89)
Act of Fear won an Edgar for the best first novel and introduces
the one-armed New York City detective, Dan Fortune.
Two seemingly simple events — the mugging of a policeman and
the disappearance of a neighbourhood youth, a possible witness
— inexorably lead Fortune to a more serious matter as one of
the witness's friends, a kid, hires Dan to find the missing boy.
Two girls, an innocent old man are murdered and Fortune's client
lands up in hospital. Then the killers go after Dan and he finds
himself in the middle of a bitter dispute between rival Mafia
factions.
"A notable writing talent" Ross Macdonald.

THREE WITH A BULLET — Arthur Lyons £2.99

A top LA music promoter hires Jacob Asch to find out who is
methodically trying to destroy him by cancelling appointments and
bookings. Then a faded superstar is found dead — apparently
from a drug overdose — and the promoter is the prime suspect.
Then two more bodies surface. Asch enters the glitzy, frenzied,
music world where the sex, drugs and rock 'n' roll combine with
ruthlessly competitive professional ambitions to create a murderous
mixture.
"Lyons writes with grace and energy" John D. MacDonald.
"Lyons belongs up there with . . . Ross Macdonald" New York
Times.
"Some of the best side of the mouth similes this side of Chandler"
Newsweek.

CASTLES BURNING — Arthur Lyons £2.99 (available 5/89)
A young L.A. artist hires Jacob Asch to track down the wife and
infant son he deserted years ago to make amends, now he has
made good. Asch finds her in the plush sybaritic world of Palm
Springs, remarried to a wealthy businessman. He finds the son
was killed in a car crash, driven by his mother. The case seems
closed until the teenage son of her second marriage is kidnapped
and Asch's client mysteriously disappears.
"Lyons writes with grace and energy" John D. MacDonald.
"Lyons belongs up there with . . . Ross Macdonald" New York
Times.
"Some of the best side of the mouth similes this side of Chandler"
Newsweek.

THE LADY IN THE MORGUE — Jonathan Latimer £3.99pb, £9.95hb

Crime was on the up. People sang of Ding-Dong Daddy, skirts were long and lives were short, violin cases mostly sported machine guns. Bill Crane thought it was a pretty wonderful time. He was in the Chicago morgue at the height of summer, trying to cool off and learn the identity of its most beautiful inmate. So-called Alice Ross had been found hanging, absolutely naked, in the room of a honky tonk hotel. His orders were to find out who she really was. Alice was stolen from her slab that night! Thus began the crazy hunt for a body and a name, through lousy hotels, dancehalls and penthouses, with occasional side trips to bed to bar to blonde and back again.

MURDER IN THE MADHOUSE — Jonathan Latimer £3.99pb, £9.95hb

Hard drinking, hard living Bill Crane in his first case has himself committed incognito to a private sanitarium for the mentally insane to protect rich, little Ms Van Camp. Terror, violence and sudden death follow when a patient is found strangled with a bathrobe cord. The murderer strikes again but makes a fatal error in killing pleasant little mute, Mr Penny. The local police doubt Crane is a bonafide detective and believe he is suffering from delusions, the non-alcoholic kind. Despite all this, Crane breaks the case in a final scene of real dramatic fury.

HEADED FOR A HEARSE — Jonathan Latimer £3.99pb, £9.95hb

Death row, Chicago county jail. Robert Westland, convicted of his wife's murder, is six days from the 'chair'. What seems an iron clad case against Westland begins to fall apart as Bill Crane races against time to investigate the background of the major players and prove Westland's innocence. Westland's two brokerage partners; his hard drinking, hard riding cousin; enigmatic and exotic Ms Brentino; the amiable Ms Hogan; a secretive clerk; a tight-lipped valet and a dipso widow all have plenty to explain. Aided by a lime squeezer, a quart of whisky, a monkey wrench, a taxi cab, a stop watch and a deep sea diver, Crane cracks the case in this locked room classic.

RED GARDENIAS — Jonathan Latimer £3.99pb,

Bill Crane's fifth and final mystery finds him teamed up again
with Doc Williams and Ann Fortune, his boss's niece, who poses
as his wife, to investigate a murder and a death threat to the
family of an industrial magnate. On the way to cracking the case
in his own, inimitable way he learns the secret of the gardenia
perfume, the lipstick marks on the dead man's face, the crimson
cat, the three shelves and the hairpin! Latimer's deft blending of
humour and suspense has been described as "masterful — the
proper proportion of dry vermouth to produce a fine martini, all
without bruising the gin!"

BLUES FOR A PRINCE — Bart Spicer £3.00pb,

The Prince was dead. Harold Morton Prince, great jazz and blues
composer had been killed in the studio of his sprawling, palatial
home. From coast to coast, the papers carried his life story and
every band was playing his blues pieces. But already ugly rumours
threatened his name. Carney Wilde, P.I., had reasons to doubt
the official story of how The Prince died and they centred on the
people closest to him: His daughter Martha, his musician
colleagues, The Prince's patient and dying father and the deadly
Hollie Gray. Threads from each of these led Wilde along the
dark road to the killer.

NO EXIT PRESS Contemporary Crime

A companion to Vintage Crime in the popular pocket book format
that highlights both the classic and exciting new books from the
past twenty years of American Crime Fiction. Contemporary Crime
will feature in 1989 such titles as Day of the Ram by William
Campbell Gault, Ask the Right Question by Michael Z Lewin,
Act of Fear by Michael Collins, Dead Ringer and Castles Burning
by Arthur Lyons all costing just £2.99.

GREEN ICE — Raoul Whitfield £3.99pb, £9.95hb

Watch out for Mal Ourney: where Mal goes, murder follows. It is on his heels as he walks out of Sing Sing after taking a manslaughter rap for a dubious dame and follows him all the way on the trail of some sizzling hot emeralds — 'Green Ice'. "naked action pounded into tough compactness by staccato, hammer-like writing" Dashiell Hammett.

DEATH IN A BOWL — Raoul Whitfield £3.99pb, £9.95hb

Maestro Hans Reiner is on the podium, taking the fiddle players through a big crescendo. Then something goes off with a bang and it isn't the tympani! Reiner finds himself with a load of lead in the back — and a new tune: The Funeral March.

THE VIRGIN KILLS — Raoul Whitfield £3.99pb, £9.95hb

Millionaire gambler Eric Vennel's yacht sets sail for the regatta at Poughkeepsie with an oddball assortment of uneasy companions: Hardheaded sportswriter Al Conners; beautiful Hollywood ham, Carla Sard; Sard's nemesis tart-tongued scribbler Rita Veld; big ugly out of place bruiser Mick O'Rourke, and a glittering cross-section of east and west coast society. Rumours of Vennel's heavy betting on the regatta and a midnight attack by a masked intruder raise the tension . . . to the point of murder!

HALO IN BLOOD — Howard Browne £3.99pb, £9.95hb

Meet Paul Pine, Chicago P.I. Three seemingly unrelated events — the funeral of a pauper at which 12 clergymen from different faiths are the only mourners; Pine being hired by John Sandmark to dig up some dirt on the man intending to marry his daughter, Leona; and a run-in with the gangster, D'Allemand, where Pine is nearly killed delivering a $25,000 ransom in counterfeit bills — are woven into a complex and web of events that produces some explosive twists to the finale.

HALO FOR SATAN — Howard Browne £3.99pb, £9.95hb.

Raymond Wirtz has something everyone wants! His grace, the Bishop of Chicago; Lola North, "a girl who could turn out to be as pure as an easter lily or steeped in sin and fail to surprise you either way"; Louis Antuni, Chicago Godfather; Constance Benbrook, who "wasn't the type to curl up with anything as inanimate as a novel" and mysterious super criminal, Jafar Baijan — all want what Wirtz has . . . the ultimate religious artefact. Private Eye, Paul Pine is right in the middle. In the middle of a deadly obstacle race strewn with corpses, cops and beautiful women.

OUT OF TIME — Michael Z. Lewin £2.99

Albert Samson feels life is looking up when he gets two clients in one afternoon. The first is an eccentric old man obsessed with his home computer who lives in an expensive apartment and asks Samson to investigate a young man suspected of running with the wrong crowd. The second is wealthy banker, Douglas A. Belter, whose wife has discovered that her birth certificate is a fake. For 48 years she has believed she is the daughter of Ella and the late Earl Wilmott Murchison. Now she wonders if she has any identity at all. Samson is intrigued by this latter case and his investigations lead him, via dusty archives, a sentimental might club owner, the police and the press, to the 1930s and '40s and to an old murder. In turn it leads Samson to suspect that a recent 'natural' death is in fact a cold blooded killing.

"Consistently readable entertainment" H. R. F. Keating, The Times.

"Very assured and satisfying" Sunday Times.

ASK THE RIGHT QUESTION — Michael Z. Lewin £2.99

When 16-year-old Eloise Crystal asks Albert Samson, an Indianapolis P.I. whose career has languished to the point of extinction to find her biological father, he's not sure whether it's a childish whim or a serious proposal. Some quick checking reveals the Crystal background to be far from crystal clear. There is the puzzling stipulation in her grandfather's will, the sudden trips her parents made to France where Eloise was conceived and to New York where she was born. Samson's digging turns up much more than a mix up in genes and he finds himself in the family closet rattling too many skeletons for his own good. ASK THE RIGHT QUESTION was an Edgar nominee for Best First Novel and introduces a detective who for sheer determination ranks with Lew Archer and Philip Marlowe.

DAY OF THE RAM — William Campbell Gault £2.50

Brock Callahan, ex guard for the L.A. Rams, is now a tough private eye, weighing in at 220 pounds with a passion for Einlicher beer. In DAY OF THE RAM, Callahan becomes involved with Johnny Quirk, ace quarterback of his old team, the Rams. Quirk fears he is being blackmailed by 'The Syndicate' into fixing the games and when Quirk turns up in the morgue, Callahan moves in to find his client's killer.

"A sharp, smooth blend of violence and murder, fashioned by one of America's most skilful mystery experts"

"Brock Callahan is a memorable believable character notable for his directness and integrity" — Art Scott.

HARD TRADE — Arthur Lyons £2.99pb
LA's most renowned detective, Jacob Asch is on the street once more in a startling tale of Californian political corruption. A troubled woman hires Asch to uncover the truth about the man she is to marry. When Asch discovers the man is gay and the woman is run down on her way to a hastily called meeting with Asch, it becomes clear something big is at stake. Serious money real estate schemes, the seamy side of LA gay life and a murder frame involve Asch in a major political scandal that costs him his licence and nearly his life.

THE KILLING FLOOR — Arthur Lyons £2.99pb
David Fein, owner of Supreme Packing, a slaughterhouse in a grimy little Californian town had a problem . . . he was a compulsive gambler. First he couldn't cover his losses from the takings so he got a loan and went into debt. By the time he took in Tortorello, a clean cut Harvard type but with 'Family' connections he was in big trouble. Now he had been missing for 4 days and his wife was frantic. Jake Bloom, old family friend puts her in touch with Jacob Asch, who figures Fein is on a bender or in the sack with another woman — he's heard and seen it all before. But that's before he finds a body on the killing floor.

DEAD RINGER — Arthur Lyons £2.99 (available 5/89)
Jacob Asch is called in by boxing promoter Jack Schwartz to help out Carlos Realango, a South American heavyweight whose career is on the skids. He has been receiving threatening phone calls and Susan Mezzano his manager and mistress thinks her husband is responsible. Asch shows them how to tap their own phone and leaves it at that. Two weeks later Asch is called to Reno to prevent Realango tearing the husband apart only to find it is too late as Realango has been shot at Moonfire ranch, a fancy brothel, owned by the husband. The police say justifiable homicide, but Asch smells murder and something more than a lovers' quarrel.
"Lyons belongs up there with . . . Ross Macdonald" New York Times.